Say Uncle

Say Uncle

Garland Stewart

iUniverse, Inc.
New York   Bloomington

iUniverse books may be ordered through booksellers or by contacting:

iUniverse
1663 Liberty Drive
Bloomington, IN 47403
www.iuniverse.com
1-800-Authors (1-800-288-4677)

Because of the dynamic nature of the Internet, any Web addresses or links contained in
this book may have changed since publication and may no longer be valid. The views
expressed in this work are solely those of the author and do not necessarily reflect the
views of the publisher, and the publisher hereby disclaims any responsibility for them.

ISBN: 978-1-4401-4991-7 (sc)
ISBN: 978-1-4401-4992-4 (dj)
ISBN: 978-1-4401-4993-1 (ebook)

Printed in the United States of America

iUniverse rev. date: 06/05/2009

1

New Light Baptist Church. A small church. My grandfather's church. Which was just outside of the town of New Hope, on this side of Rose Hill, Mississippi and about a forty minute drive from our house. He'd been pastor here for over twenty-five years. I grew up in this church; I was baptized in the creek behind the Home of Grace Men's Shelter which was about a half a mile down the road.

We got to church just as the service was about to start at 11 a.m.; I couldn't handle Sunday School, so we didn't even try to make that. Mamma went in first, carrying Allie. Then Trisha, Megan and Caleb followed them in. I brought up the rear holding Diane. Everyone turned and watched us go to the second pew where my grandmother had already staked out a claim. Grandma never sat on the first pew in front because she felt that would be "prideful" and would take too much advantage of her relationship with grandpa. But everybody knew who was in charge of that relationship. It could be summed up by looking at their checking accounts; his checking account was their checking account, but her checking account was her checking account. Mamma sat next to her, and I sat at the other end of the pew, near the aisle.

"It does my heart good to see so many fresh faces, many of whom we haven't seen in a while," grandpa said, not looking in my direction at all because that would be too obvious. He had always personified religion for me; he was big and gruff and had an enigmatic face. *"Let us bow our heads and pray."*

I didn't bow my head. I never had. I remember as a child thinking that if I wanted to talk to god and god was in heaven then I should look up. Grandpa and I got into a major disagreement over this; he said that bowing showed that we were subservient to god's will. I really didn't like being subservient.

He finished praying and continued, "*Today, my brothers and sisters, I would like for us to look at Luke, chapter 15, verse 11. The Parable of the lost son.*" The Prodigal Son. He still didn't look at me, but I had to nod to myself. He was good. I put a semi-smile on my face and prepared to nod encouragingly every once in a while, trying to remember how I amused myself in this church as a child. My attention span has always been kind of free flowing, tidal-like; I'd think about something then hear a snippet of sermon then I'd think about something else. It's a handy skill to have. I took a deep breath and made sure my smile was nailed in place; preparing myself mentally to accept whatever it took to be brought back into the fold, the acrid scent of my burnt bridges still heavy in the air.

"*And so the younger son said to his father, 'I want my share of the estate.' So the father divided all that he owned between them.*"

It wasn't supposed to happen this way. There was a plan. A good plan. The minute, the very nanosecond I graduated from college I knew I would shake the Mississippi mud off of my shoes and never live in this state again. And that's exactly what I did. I accepted a job teaching English as a Second Language to military students in Saudi Arabia working for the Ministry of Defense and Aviation. I had never been on a plane. I had never been further north than Memphis, Tennessee or further east than Tuscaloosa, Alabama. My family was not thrilled that I was going to another continent especially one in which another religion (Islam) was in the majority. My grandmother said she was worried about my immortal soul; she'd always been worried about my soul. And even then she had been saying we were living in the "end of days" for as long as I could remember. She kissed me and said, "You be careful in that Saudi Arabia, you hear me? It's near Nicaragua." Then she said, "It's a good thing you're going. You can minister to them and tell them about Jesus Christ, Our Lord and Savior and bring them into the fold. He is the staff of comfort." Her eyes lit up like I was going to fight in the Crusades. I kept quiet; I just wanted a job out of Mississippi. Plus I didn't think I'd be the best purveyor of anything spiritual. My grandfather didn't say anything. He and I still weren't talking at the time either; he was worried about my soul too but for a completely different reason.

When I got my first call back from Major Al-Turki in the Royal Saudi Embassy in Washington, D.C., I hung up on him because I thought my friends were playing a joke on me. I mean, who could be named Al Turkey? But they were desperate for teachers, and I was desperate for a job that paid more than minimum wage. Plus, it sounded really cool. Major Al-Turki (when he finally called back and convinced me that he was a real person trying to offer me a job) asked me if I'd ever been to the kingdom of Saudi Arabia before.

"No," I replied.

"You'll be working in the south in the mountains. In a place called Taif," he gushed, "It's just like Switzerland."

"Hmmm," I thought, "that might be nice." I'd never been to Europe. I signed a two year contract; they sent me a ticket. I got a passport, loaded up and headed out with exactly $32 in my pocket. My first year there, I made more money than my mother who had worked at the same company for over twenty years. Just under $60,000 a year, tax-free to work from 8 a.m. until 2 p.m. Saturday through Wednesday (the weekend is Thursday and Friday); there were also a lot of holidays.

"Not too long after that, the young man set off for a distant land and led an awful lifestyle, squandering his wealth in debauchery and wild living."

The first and second contracts were wonderful. I traveled all over Asia, Africa and Europe, including Switzerland which I might add was nothing like Taif, Saudi Arabia.

The third contract was okay. This was about the time of the first Gulf War. I couldn't help but admire the irony of the situation. My family had always told me I needed to join the military, but I couldn't think of anything I'd rather do less. And here I was in a war zone watching the windows to see if any Scud missiles were landing that day and trying to find duck tape (that's what I thought it was really called), not quite sure what for but I'd heard it might be needed, and it gave me focus.

The language barrier proved a tad insurmountable as I would go into the veiled-mom and pop stores in the souk --market-- and say really slowly, "Duck tape?" and smile really big. I even tried to walk like a duck – it seemed logical at the time; it never occurred to me that they might call it something else that had nothing to do with ducks. That being said, I did seem to greatly amuse any bystanders; I think some of them really knew what I was talking about but wanted to see this crazy American quack and walk around with arms folded and flapping although this performance led to at least two invitations from the veiled-moms and pops for dinner. General Ahmad Hilal, the head of the base where I worked, called off all vacations when the war started, saying that our "expertise might be essential in the war effort." Me. Helping with the war effort. I guess I could have stood out in the desert and hurled conjugated verbs at the enemy. Suddenly I pictured myself hiding behind a sand dune with a regiment of enemy soldiers marching by and me popping up and yelling, "Hide!" and going back down. Then coming back up on the other side of the dune to shout, "Hid!" and then dropping to the ground, crawling to another dune and yelling, "Hidden!!" I could see me putting the fear of god or allah into them. I giggled and someone in the pew in front of me looked back at me and made a shushing motion.

"After he had spent everything, there was a famine in that distant land and the young man began to be in need."

The last contract was awful. Anti-American sentiment was running pretty high. Many of my students who had just returned from sitting in bunkers on the Iraqi and Kuwaiti borders insisted that Saudi "hadn't really needed American help and could have defeated Saddam alone." I didn't mention that before the war, many of them weren't even allowed to have bullets in their very large, expensive guns – they tended to hurt themselves or shoot straight up in the air when they were excited (which unfortunately led to many deaths when the bullets came back down). Plus, it was getting pretty dangerous for Americans in general.

The final straw for me was when I was walking to town from the compound where I lived (about a ten minute walk), and a group of kids in the back of a pick up truck that had to be going at least 60 mph threw rocks at me – though it was difficult to estimate their speed as I was trying to bob and weave- and yelled Arabic obscenities like

"Fuck your mother," "In Your Ass," or (my favorite) "Your Sister's Ugly" which not only implies that your sister is ugly but also that she was immodest enough to show her face – it's an honor thing that gets lost in translation. It was time to leave. I was planning to return home for, what I considered, a much needed vacation and then continue traveling around the world, teaching to pay the bills and earn money. Actually, I had my eyes on Oman and teaching at the Sultan Qaboos University. Then I'd have many of the perks without the restrictions of Saudi society which is basically run on the premise that if something is fun or interesting, it must be from the devil and is therefore forbidden. Almost exactly like Mississippi.

"And the young man thought to himself that he was not worthy to be called son by his father; maybe he could return to his father's house to be a hired man."

Right after my stoning, my mother called to tell me she was having carpal tunnel surgery on both of her arms. She had put if off as long as she could (against the doctor's advice) and could put it off no longer. It was time to come home. I could help my mother during her recovery, relax a bit, then be on my way. Or so I thought. I didn't know how bad things were until I got home. Mamma had put off her surgery because she had to watch my sister's kids. Lynn would drop them off and disappear for weeks at a time. I had heard some of this but had only gotten the sanitized version that is given to all people who "aren't here." When I talked to my mother, she would mention something or other, and I would spout all sorts of advice and move on to the next topic. I was a great, most knowledgeable spouter, and my mother in her infinite wisdom just thanked me and didn't say anything else. That's my mom. She would literally do anything up to and including hurting herself for her family. She had not mentioned the downward spiral my sister Lynn was in, possibly because it caused her so much pain. I really don't know why she didn't say anything to me about it. But I got home and found Mamma sick and trying to squeeze Trisha (9), Megan (6), Caleb (3), Allie (2), and Diane (6 weeks) all into Mamma's too-small, three bedroom house.

"The son cried to his father, 'I have sinned against heaven and against you. I'm not worthy to be called your son.'"

One of the investments I had made while working overseas was to buy a house (for $35,000 – I thought I was such an astute businessman) two blocks from my mother and across the street and two houses down from my grandparents. The house actually had three apartments in it, and I had originally planned to live in one and rent out the others to give me extra cash while I was doing time in Mississippi, thus keeping me from dipping into savings. That idea didn't last long. After the surgery, while she was convalescing, I saw how things really were. The kids didn't ever want to go home with their mother.

When they did go, they came back dirty and hungry and somehow empty, a hollowness around the edges that I couldn't quite identify. Trisha told me that she had watched her mother smoke a rock and once, while we were watching television, pictures of the most wanted criminals in the area came on the screen; Trisha looked up at the t.v. and said that one of them looked "just like the man mamma was always giving money to."

Social services was just about to take the kids away from Lynn; they had already investigated her once and left with a "revisit within 60 days" notice. I couldn't just walk away. But it was just like being in Saudi Arabia and anxiously watching the windows for Scud missiles – I knew something was coming; I just didn't know what. My mother was going to take on those kids no matter what, and she really wasn't able to.

So I there I was, back in the one place I swore I would never live in again. Working hard to rebuild those bridges I'd torched. Trying to calculate exactly how many services I would have to attend to get back into my grandparents' good graces. Applying duck tape to my life.

"And the father said, 'It is right that we celebrate; he was lost but now is found.'"

2

I am not a hero. Never have been. First, I don't like tights. And I whine too much. Plus, I'm tired. And lonely. And very depressed. And overdrawn. Kids will do that to you. One kid's bad enough; five is just crazy. And they're not even mine. Well, not technically. Those kids weren't the reason I returned to Mississippi, but they were the reason I stayed.

"I need seven dollars to go skating Friday."

"I need twenty-two dollars for cheerleading."

"The prom is in two weeks – it's twenty-five dollars to get in. And guess what? There's a dress on sale at Dillard's for ninety-nine dollars."

"I got 40 boxes of chocolate – can you take them to sell at work?"

"Look! The girl scout cookies came! You owe sixty dollars."

God must have had a plan, but I sure didn't know what it was. And he had a lot to answer for. My list of questions started with "What were you thinking?" and meandered through "Why me?" and just petered out with a rousing "Fuck you!" I knew the answer, mostly: because there was no one else. My mother couldn't do it, at least not alone. I couldn't do it alone either. No one else was willing. Alone, neither of us was capable. Together, maybe. Sometimes those life altering decisions aren't decisions at all. They're necessities standing there staring you down, daring you to blink and look away. The people around me loved to hear stories about the children ("What did you and yo Mamma do when Megan put the car in drive and went through the fence at the Piggly Wiggly?"), but that's all it was for those who could escape back to their normal lives. A funny anecdote concealing absolute desperation wrapped in a sphincter clinching sort of terror. My desperation. My terror. Homegrown. But they didn't see that. Or the insanity at the core of my humor. Or the tears. They didn't see the tears. No one did. Those were private, almost sacred and full of guilt.

Mamma, trying to be reassuring, said, "You're still young; you'll find someone to love," then, "go whip Caleb – he said 'shit' again."

The man at the food stamp office with a What Would Jesus Do bracelet on his wrist said, "You own a car and have a house – application denied." The security officer at the food stamp office pointed through the window to the parking lot and showed me women with perfectly coiffed hair and meticulous nails who got their food stamps (because they didn't have cars or houses) and immediately ran out and gave them over to their drug dealers (who were probably renting too).

Grandma said, "Put fifty dollars a month in savings so it'll be there when you need it, and ya'll won't always run out of food."

Grandpa once said, "Don't ever come here again. You're not welcome in my house."

The policeman said, "Your mother knowingly wrote bad checks. Pay for court costs and, if she promises not to do it again, she gets two years probation."

My sister, Lynn, said, "I gotta live my life. And kids ain't in it. I just drink a little and I don't inject nothing. Now get the Hell out of my house."

My other sister, Sara, said, "He only hit me once; I'm not getting a divorce. I love him."

The lady at the checkout said, "Your card has been declined. Do you have another form of payment?"

Grandpa just said, "I have cancer again. Can you take me to the doctor?"

Mamma said, "Doing the right thing ain't ever easy." And the easy way is rarely right. I got it.

The man in a green jacket, a Gideon, said, "Would you like a copy of the New Testament? It'll bring you closer to Jesus." Oh goody.

Take a deep breath. Breathe in. Deep. Deeper, until I thought my chest would explode, taking my head and heart with it. Hold it. Let it suck up all of the anxiety and ugliness in my mind and soul and world. Now let it out, slowly. So slowly. I smiled, feeling lightheaded.

A student wrote on my evaluation, "Mr. Stewart is sexy. He should teach naked."

I prayed. Sort of. Al Anon says to pray to the God of Your Understanding. That was a laugh. I didn't know the god of my understanding. We diverged a while back. Around the time I acquired the kids. Around the time my world broke and reality seeped in in the form of a drug dealer named Fontaine who called to tell me to come get them because my sister Lynn was unconscious on the floor and Diane's diaper needed changing, and he "watn't gonna change no fucking diaper." It was cold, the coldest we'd had in a while. And there was no food. After we got them home and safely in bed, I walked down the hallway, out the back door and down the stairs to the laundry room that stood next to the gate. I went in and closed the door and cried, trying to empty my soul of the spiked lump that had been growing there since I got back home. A lump that somehow encompassed all of my life. Thirty one years that had mostly been all mine. My world. The cry got stuck in my throat, tangled with the lump in my soul, and every bit of energy I had left me; I collapsed against the wall, pressing my forehead against the cold, rough stone and listening to a pair of tennis shoes in the dryer: hating my sister, thwump, hating Mississippi, thwump, thwump, hating reality, thwump, thwump, thwump, hating god. Even as I was forced to thank him for getting me and my mother there and letting the kids be alright. But that was all god was going to get from me. Breathe. Let it all draw out. Nothing but a hollow space left. I didn't want kids. Four girls and a boy. Good kids. Relatively. I didn't want them. They were not easy. Reality never is.

"Look at me when I'm talking to you!" I said, grabbing Allie's arm. "Don't hit him again!"

"I didn't," she said, brown eyes wide with innocence.

I see a red hand print just her size on Caleb's back. "Then, how'd that get there?" I said, pointing to his back.

"I don't know," she answered with that same guileless look.

Shit.

The window of my car falls down. The electric motor in the driver's door gave a final groan last month and burned out just at almost the exact time Megan's orthodontist bill was due. So the window falls down. Very slowly unless I hit bumps. Then swoosh! I have a Master's Degree. In English Literature. And I drive down the interstate with one hand on the steering wheel and the other holding my window up. I shove pieces of paper in the corner to keep it up during the day. The window stayed up but then everything else seemed to fall down. And there just weren't enough pieces of paper.

"Do you have any weapons on board?"

"I beg your pardon?"

"Weapons. Sir, please roll your window down."

"I can't. If I let it go down, I can't get it back up," I said pointing to the piece of paper (as if that explained everything).

He sighed, then placed a very-put-upon-smile on his face, "Any guns or knives?"

"No." At least I hoped not; I never know what the kids might leave in the car.

"Have a nice day, sir."

This was when I taught at the Navy Base which is about twenty-five miles outside of town. On Monday and Wednesday nights for eight weeks. English Composition.

My boss had said, "Teach this class. You'll like the base. The class is small. The students are better. Two nights a week from 5-7:40pm." An extra class. That means more money.

"Pull under the awning, sir." I got checked every time I came to the base. I am the nerdiest of the nerds (one of my students said, "Mr. Stewart, you are just too white."), but obviously to these *nice* soldier guys I looked like a terrorist. My roommate when I worked overseas had this problem. Every time he went through airport security, he was frisked and given a body cavity search. He complained about it once and was shown pictures of the top ten terrorists in the world; he looked like all of them. And that was before 9/11.

"Okay," I said, trying to look as non-threatening as possible.

"Step out of the car and open the doors, the hood, and the trunk."

"How do you open the hood?"

"I don't know, sir; I can't touch the car." I pulled the lever for the trunk, found the lever for the hood ("I'll bet this happens all the time" – "No, sir") and opened all four doors.

"What's this, sir?" Corporal Something asked in a tone that inspired confidence and allayed all fears.

"Part of a jelly donut. Looks like blueberry." We hadn't had jelly donuts for four months. That was what I'd been smelling.

"Thank you, sir. Have a nice day."

I got home by 8:15 p.m. The kids were bathed and ready for bed; thank god.

"Who left the jelly donut in the back floorboard of my car?"

Diane said, "Caleb."

"Did you see him?"

"No."

"Then how do you know he did it?" I asked, having learned never to take things at face value.

"He likes jelly donuts."

"So do you."

"But I eat all of mine. 'Cept the blueberry ones – they're nasty."

My boss said, "Would you like to teach an extra class at Lost Gap?"

"Sure." More money. Nothing was like I thought it'd be; nothing was cheap and my savings had been punctured in at least eighteen places.

Later, another teacher said, "I can't believe you're teaching at the prison."

"Who's teaching at a prison?" I asked, knowing that no one in his right mind would agree to that.

"You are. Lost Gap is that new prison just outside of town."

Oh. I thought it was some sort of satellite campus. Get the newbie to teach; he'll teach anywhere. The teaching whore. No, whores give it away; I'm a teaching prostitute.

"Karen, you give the G.E.D. out at the prison, right? How is it?"

"It's okay," she said, thought about it a bit more, then added, "Just ignore the prisoners."

"What's to ignore?"

"Sometimes they're *really* glad to see you."

"That's just the women though, right?"

"Don't be too sure. You're pretty cute. And more than a little sexy. Like I said, ignore them. Gwen didn't. She says she won't go back." She stopped and looked at me intensely. "You don't get cable, do you?"

"Yeah, why?"

"Don't watch any of those damned prison dramas. At least not until you've been there a few times."

"Hey Gwen," I said, catching up to her on the sidewalk, "You went to the prison to give the G.E.D. test, didn't you?"

"Don't get me started about that place. You know it's for psychologically disturbed inmates."

This just gets better and better. Repeat the mantra: I need the money, I need the money. "No, I didn't know that. I'm supposed to teach an English class there."

"Why would they want to learn English? Most of 'em are gonna be there a very long while. This place will do anything for money. Well, you have fun! I won't go back."

"Why not?"

"The last time I went, an inmate wrote me a note," she said and shuddered, "It was horrible."

"What did it say?"

"I can't repeat it. I was sexually harassed, and I wasn't even cute that day."

"You think they'll enjoy writing essays?" I asked hopefully.

Push button. Buzz open. Clang.

"Always make sure the door is closed securely behind you. We usually give a two hour orientation when people first start working here," said the burly no-nonsense corrections officer.

"I didn't get an orientation," I pointed out.

"I know. There wasn't time. Here's one of our pamphlets." He handed me a very glossy pamphlet with a glorious facility on the front, very photogenic guards and multi-ethnic prisoners who must have been framed because they couldn't possibly be hardened criminals. "Just don't do anything you might regret."

"Like what?"

"They go over that in the orientation."

"Which I didn't get."

"Don't worry. All of the rooms in this facility are controlled from Central Command." He pointed to a large red button on the right. "Press this button and Central will open the door for you. They keep tabs on what's going on – wait a minute." We walked through the doors, pulled them closed; then he looked down at his clipboard, pursed his lips and cleared his throat. "Ummm. This is your room." He pointed to the left. The room was next to the cafeteria. "There is one room that can't be controlled by central and has to be opened manually," he took out a key and opened the door, holding it open for me to go inside. "It's also the biggest classroom."

"My room isn't controlled from central command?" I said, feeling the beginnings of a sharp pain in my stomach and a tightening of my chest.

"We've never had a problem."

"How long have you been here?"

"About four months, since the place opened. I'll send the students down. You have twelve, I believe. Don't close the door completely, or it'll lock and only a couple of us have keys." He turned to leave.

"Wait. What do I do if it does lock?"

"Just get my attention." He pointed to the two windows in the classroom which looked out onto a hallway that was big enough to march at least four shackled prisoners down and had a podium perched somewhat menacingly in the middle of it even further down the hall – practically in Canada. "And I'll come and open it."

"You'll be at the podium the whole time?"

"When I'm not on rounds."

Wonderful.

"My name is Garland Stewart, and for the next eighteen weeks I'll be teaching you English." Nothing. Lots of stripes, green and white, black and white. No red and white. The two prisoners who were wearing red and white were being led down the hall in chains. I guess they had better things to do than learn English.

"I hope you like the course. I want ya'll to do a sample writing so I can see what your ability is. It will help me determine what we need to work on." No response. Lots of tattoos. Frayed looking tattoos. Maybe homemade? One student, I think his name was Valencia, had perfectly plucked eyebrows, and was wearing sandals; his toenails were painted red. "Why are all of you taking this class?" No sound except the racket of the lunch crowd next door and the whoosh of air going through the classroom. Then the unmistakable clink of the door closing and locking. I'm gonna die.

"Mr. Stewart?"

"Yes?"

"This is a real college class, right?"

"Yes. Exactly the same as the one on campus." Except for the bars, and the guards with pepper spray, and the locked doors. "You get three credit hours." Where's that guard? I went and stood next to the window so that they would at least see any blood as I'm stabbed to death by the pencils and pens I had just given my class. Be nonchalant. Be their friend, so they won't kill you. "Are you trying to get your Associate's degree?"

"Hell, I'll be able to get my doctorate by the time I get outta this place."

"Good, Marlon isn't it?"

"Yep, you alright? You don't look so good."

"I'm okay. I was just wondering where that guard was."

"Henderson don't come around here much."

"He said he makes rounds."

"Those can take anywhere from twenty minutes to two hours."

Great. Maybe there'll be something left to identify.

"Mr. Stewart?" This from red toenails.

"Yes?"

"Do you ever watch General Hospital?"

I had a dream. Once, a long time ago. I would travel the world teaching English and make lots of money. It came true for eight years. Then I woke up. In prison. Teaching.

"No, you like that soap opera?"

"Valencia gets fashion tips from the soaps," said a guy (Jajuan?) with a Star of David on his forearm and a teardrop under his left eye.

"Bite my ass twice," said Valencia with just a hint of a grin, obviously renewing a previous conversation.

"Jus' name the time and the place," said Jajuan. He had two gold teeth in front. One had a capital J on it. He reminded me of a professor I had had in college.

"Third World would kill you. And me too." Third World? Boyfriend? Pedicurist?

"He don't have to know." He smiled playfully and grabbed his crotch. "'Sides, it's my birthday."

"Say doesn't not don't," I said before I remembered where I am. Always a teacher even in the face of death. Tomorrow's headline: *Teacher Dies Promoting Subject-Verb Agreement; He Was Warned in the Orientation!* Jajuan didn't seem to mind; in fact, he nodded his thanks, and for some reason, I was oddly comforted and the tightening of my chest eased a bit, so I continued, "Take out a pen and piece of paper and let's get started. I want you to write a paragraph about what you hope to get out of this class." I knew what I wanted – freedom and solid colors. But while I was waiting, maybe I should continue standing next to the window and look for Henderson and that key.

3

Having children meant I had to be less selfish which was not my natural state. Being single and opinionated, I spewed wisdom like a fountain, and, like any good fountain, I kept none for myself. I had always been one of these people who would see a child throwing a tantrum in a store and immediately blame the parent: "If that were my child, I'd snatch him up and beat him 'til he couldn't walk!" These words came back to haunt me with a vengeance. We rented out my mother's house and opened up all of the apartments in mine. The kids took to the new house with great verve and vigor. It was an old house two stories high with a great big staircase running down the center. I had the kitchens taken out of two of the apartments and had some other things done (the bare minimum needed for safety). The house was huge. Five bedrooms and three bathrooms. The kids were used to living in a small trailer way out in the country, so they ran and played all over the house all day. They loved it. That was not, however, the way they felt about me. I was an unknown who appeared in their midst with lots of opinions about the way things should be done, most of which were wrong.

I didn't like having to take Caleb to the bathroom with me so "he could learn to pee standing up." It seemed to take him forever to get the hang of it, and he'd started kind of late anyway. Plus I felt distinctly uncomfortable with the entire process. And when he did start peeing and pooping in his potty, every adult in what seemed like a ten mile radius had to run into the bathroom and applaud - the same was done for Allie and Diane – the applauding, not the learning to pee standing up. And for a while, Allie tried to pee outside like Caleb and couldn't understand why her pee went straight down and not on the tree like his. She and Caleb would go to the bathroom together; Caleb on the toilet and Allie on the potty chair even though she really didn't understand what we wanted her to do. Caleb would sit down and yell, "Come push my wee wee down!" Pretty soon, Allie would do the same, so that when I came in to push Caleb's wee wee down, I'd also have to pretend to push hers down too. Good times.

Caleb and I didn't get along from almost the first moment we were in the same proximity. Here we were, two alpha males squaring off, vying for position. After we'd been in the house a few months, I remember putting him in the bathtub in the back bathroom on the first floor directly across the hall from the kitchen. He loved bubbles, so I made sure that there were lots of bubbles in the water. Then I went across the hall to get a cup of coffee. I was not over there but a minute and heard the doorbell ring. I made my way to the front door, yelling over my shoulder to Caleb, "You better wash behind those ears, ya hear? I'll be checking." The front door had a large glass oval in the middle of it, and through that I saw a dark blue minivan in the driveway. A strange middle aged, well dressed woman was outside the door on the porch. I opened the door, and she said in a very condescending tone, "Is this child yours?" And there was Caleb, naked, covered in bubbles. The lady said, "I found him running down the road." That pretty much sums up my parenting skills.

Because I don't like to be touched myself, I never really liked touching the kids. I was too distant; I don't know why or I couldn't admit the reason then. I hugged and kissed them more out of a sense of duty than anything else. I would mentally run through my list of things to do: shave? check, bathe? check, hug kids? check check check check check.

I made them talk when they clearly didn't want to and didn't listen when they needed to talk. I was still mourning the loss of my old life, and I took it out on them. I paddled Megan when she wet the bed, making her feel worse than she already did. I wouldn't let her drink anything after seven and continually fussed at her. She would just look at me and take whatever I dished out quietly. I paddled Caleb because he ran away from Little People Day Care every day; he tried to disappear into an empty lot right next door that had a lot of trees, jumping out of the car as soon as it stopped and grabbing a tree. We then would have to pry his hands away from the tree. And he would do that any time the staff took the kids outside. They charged us extra for that child. I think I would have tried to paddle both Allie's and Diane's diaper covered behinds too if I could have. I would yell about something, and my mother would look at me as if to ask how I could become so angry over something so insignificant.

I was an abuser. It never occurred to me that they might be nervous about living in a new house, nervous about living with me, worried about their mother. And, of course, I missed all of the signs. Every time they went anywhere, Trisha and Megan had a ritual – that was eventually picked up by all of the others; they would say, "You're my Baby, you're my baby doll, you're my best friend, bye, I love you." And Mamma and I had to dutifully listen and then kiss them at least three or four times each. They were old enough to worry about Lynn. And she soothed her conscience by calling the children (even then, only occasionally) to tell them how much she loved them and they would still be with her except Mamma and I wouldn't let her have them. But she really had no where to bring them; she'd lost the trailer and gone through a succession of progressively worse boyfriends – the last having gone out for bread and never returned.

Then there were the other issues. Caleb's feet started turning inward badly, so he had to wear special, super expensive shoes that would turn them out. They were these very hard shoes that angled out at about thirty degrees and had a steel rod connecting them and keeping them angled. We had to put them on him after he was asleep and fight with him all night to keep them on. Megan had to have surgery to have sinus passages drilled in her head.

Mamma was wonderful through all of it. Sitting in the hospital, reading a book, so very good in a crisis. I, on the other hand, was exactly the opposite. Trisha had a lazy eye. She'd had to wear special glasses since she was about two -or was supposed to wear the glasses; Lynn was notoriously untrustworthy about those kinds of things. And Trisha was always so cute with her blonde hair and huge blue eyes. Once she reached a certain age (ten, I think), she needed surgery to correct the problem. The surgery was in Jackson, which is about an hour and fifteen minute drive away, so the other kids had to stay with my grandparents. Since she had to be at the outpatient clinic by 6 am, Mamma, Trisha, and I drove over the night before and stayed in a hotel. We got her to the clinic dutifully at the appointed time; she took a pregnancy test (when she heard that she had to do this Trisha said, "I don't even have a boyfriend!" but the nurse still insisted as they had had a problem with a pregnant nine year old the month before), and Mamma and I waited patiently in the waiting room. A couple of hours later the doctor came out and said everything had gone well and Trisha had woken up and we could go back and see her. She was sitting upright in a recliner, and I couldn't help but notice that there were these suture things coming out of her right eye (the one being operated on). My first reaction was "Hey, you left something out!" I think I even said that. The doctor laughed and said, "No, I have to make adjustments after she is completely awake." I didn't like the sound of that at all. The doctor then faced Trisha, put his left thumb on her right eyeball and started pulling the sutures to "make the adjustments." I fainted. Dead away. I woke up a few minutes later in my own recliner. Right next to Trisha's. I made it all the way through the Gulf War, but I couldn't deal with a little eye surgery.

Lynn never called to see how Trisha was doing. I don't think she even knew Trisha was having surgery.

4

The exceedingly polite police officer at my front door said he had a warrant for my mother's arrest. It was a Thursday afternoon; Mamma had laid down with Caleb, Allie and Diane for a nap. I'd been reading in the living room. Trisha and Megan were somewhere upstairs. My sister Sara was in the kitchen making sandwiches for her and her daughter Mckenna. They'd been staying over a lot lately because she and her husband were having trouble. I heard the doorbell and then I heard Trisha yell, "The police are outside!" I got to the door, and I saw the police car in the driveway. Every time I see police or police cars, I mentally go through my mind and try to think of anything that I could have done that might be construed as being illegal. I was in the clear as far as I knew, so I opened the door. They didn't want me; they wanted my mother.

Not having a clue what to do, I called Mamma; she came to the door, followed by Caleb and Allie. Diane had fallen asleep. Mckenna and Sara had come from the kitchen, Sara still carrying her sandwich. Trisha and Megan were watching from the top of the stairs. The police officer repeated to Mamma that he had a warrant for her arrest.

"What is this about?" I asked him, although I meant it for my mother.

"I don't know," she said, getting visibly nervous. Her eyes got a distant look in them and glazed over; she seemed to shut down, not answering any other questions.

"Mamma?" I asked. She still didn't answer, so I turned back to the police officer.

"When do you have to take her?"

"Now," he replied. "She'll be arraigned downtown."

"For what?" I asked, knowing that all of the neighbors would be looking out of their windows by now. And my grandparents. Oh god.

"Uttering," he said tonelessly, looking at the warrant.

"Does she have to go in the police car? Can I bring her down?"

"We have to bring her in," he said, then added apologetically, "And we're going to have to handcuff her."

Mamma said nothing as they handcuffed her, led her down the steps from the front porch, and put her into the back of their car. She just sat there, staring at a vague nothingness in front of her as they backed out of the driveway and drove away, leaving the rest of us standing on the front porch.

"What is uttering?" Sara asked.

"I think it's talking bad about someone," I said, thinking that it was talking under your breath, no that's muttering, then I continued, "Watch the kids. I gotta go find out what's going on."

I got to the police station very quickly, ran in, went through security and was escorted back to the jail. I told the uniformed lady behind the glass what I was doing there.

She nodded her head, buzzed me in and said, "I don't think yo Mamma is feeling the best in the world." She took me into a small room with a little table and a large man sitting behind it.

Mr. Stewart," he said immediately, "I'm handling your mother's case." If he said a name, I don't remember it. Everything was on Speed. "Your mother has been charged with uttering."

"Who did she talk about?"

He stared at me for a long moment and said, "Uttering is knowingly writing bad checks."

"No. That can't be right," I insisted. He put a piece of paper in front of me. There was a list of places and dates and amounts. Piggly Wiggly, Winn Dixie, Walmart, Save-a-lot, CVS drugstore, some bulk meat place. Great. This was how we'd been fed. The dates showed about two years worth. Even some Christmas stuff. I started rubbing my neck and asked, "How much is the total?"

"Almost $3,000. A felony."

"Oh god."

"I've tried to talk to her but she seems a bit out of sorts. I understand she's under a doctor's care. And on a good bit of medication."

"Yeah." Her pain had been getting really bad lately. I didn't see how she could take any of it and still function. The week before, I hurt my back and she gave me one of her pills. I halfed it and then halfed it again. I still slept for two days.

"If she makes restitution and pays court costs, there will be no jail time. But she will be put on probation."

"How much does she owe?"

He looked at another paper in his folder and said, "$5,327.53, total. Can she pay it?"

I knew she didn't have any money. I still had almost $6,000 in savings, so I said, "Yeah."

"Good. When?"

"Right now," I said, pulling out my check book.

He looked at it and then at me, "I think we're gonna need cash from your family."

"Fine," I said, "let me run to the bank."

After I returned from the bank and paid cash, my mother was brought out. She was so pale her skin was translucent. She still didn't say anything and had to be directed to sit in the other chair by the nice police lady, who sat her down, patted her arm, and said, "There, there honey." We got her to sign papers saying she was guilty. Then she had to sign her probation papers. Two years of probation. If she wrote anything bad in that time, she'd go to jail for five to seven years. And leave me alone with all of those children.

I got her up so we could go and get her purse and get out of that place.

"Mr. Stewart?" I looked at him, and he continued, "You better keep an eye on yo mama."

5

Money. Our situation was getting desperate. After the renovations to the house(which ran into some structural issues – who knew a house had to be "level"?), the various illnesses, and Mamma's run in with the law, there was definitely more outgo than income. As much as I hated to admit it, I needed a job. Because I had taught English as a Second Language in Saudi Arabia and was very impressed with my own credentials, I went to the local community college, my alma mater, to see if there was anything I could teach. The place had not changed at all. There were signs advertising free lunch on Wednesdays furnished by the Baptist Student Union but only if you listened to the sermon first. And there were nice Gideons in their bright green jackets; they came to campus at the beginning and end of each semester to hand out new testaments. I had collected four just walking across campus. I had learned a long time ago that if you refused to take one from them, you set yourself up for a very long winded speech, so I took whatever they handed out and smiled; I was wondering what to do with them when I ran into my old Western Civilization teacher Dr. Dennis who just happened to be the Dean of Academic Affairs. We talked for a bit, and she was very encouraging. She called me the next day and asked me to come to her office because she had something she wanted to discuss. I got there, and she said excitedly, "You have an interview with Dr. Ryan, the vice president of the college!"

"Hunh?" I asked intelligently, happy that I'd worn slacks and not the jeans I almost put on.

"Dr. Ryan," she repeated. "I told him about you, and he agreed to talk to you. It might lead to a faculty position."

"I really wish you'd mentioned this on the phone."

"I didn't want you to be nervous."

"Thanks," I said, "But if I'd known, I'd have dressed better. I thought I was just seeing you; I just wanted to be clean. This is not interview attire." I waved my hand from my shirt to my pants for emphasis.

"Oh pooh! You look fine. But you better go now; he's expecting you."

I walked over to the administration building, tucking my shirt a little more in my belt and trying to brush the wrinkles out of my allegedly wrinkle-free Dockers. I got to his office and was immediately ushered into another office by a very efficient secretary.

"Dr. Ryan?"

"Yeah," he said brusquely, "have a seat," pointing to an empty chair. He was a thin, balding man with large glasses and even larger frown lines. "Dr. Dennis has a lot of good things to say about you."

"She's really nice." I said, smiling.

"She's says you've traveled a lot." Then he leaned forward, his hands clasped together on his desk, "You don't have any infectious ideas, do you?"

"No," I said slowly, thinking that he must have meant infectious diseases but not wanting to correct someone who might give me a job. "I was sprayed in Customs," and I smiled even bigger, trying to make a joke out of it. He exhaled slowly, leaning back in his chair.

"Right," he pursed his lips, "We need a teacher. Dr. Dennis says you'll do. You will teach Developmental English and Speech." He put his hand over his mouth, ruminating, then dropped it and continued, "And I'm gonna ask you, and this is strictly voluntary, mind you, but we need an advisor for the Black Student Association. You think you could do that?"

"Yes, sir," I said, needing a job. Black Student Association Advisor? Great.

"Alright," he wrote something on a piece of paper and pushed it across the desk to me, "This is what we're prepared to offer you. Non-negotiable." I looked at the paper. $14, 000. He definitely wasn't impressed with my credentials. But it was more than I was making now, and at least it would cover utilities and food.

"Okay," I said.

"Good. Come back tomorrow to sign your contract," he said dismissively. I got up and went to the door.

"And Mr. Stewart?" I turned back to him.

"Make sure you volunteer in a timely fashion."

I went back to Dr. Dennis' office.

"Well, how'd it go?" she asked.

"Okay, I guess. He offered me a job."

"See? I told you everything would be okay."

"Yeah. Did you mention to him that I really needed a job?" I had confided in her about all of my fears, both about the kids and about money.

"I might have. But don't you worry. We're one big happy family here."

I signed the contract the next day and then was told that I would be teaching a class over the summer. On Tuesday and Thursday nights. The head of the English department, a wonderful woman, gave me a sample syllabus, the book, and a few other things she felt I might need. I went home and organized everything and decided how and when I would do this and that. I felt in complete control as I strolled (strutted) into the classroom that first Tuesday night, introducing myself and telling the students in very general terms what was expected. Then I held up the book for the course, and I heard a general murmur coming from them.

A student at the front said, "This is the book they gave us in the bookstore." And he held up his book which was not anything like mine. I had been given the wrong book. There went my strut. Picking up whatever pieces I could (of my dignity as well as of the lecture), I improvised, deciding to do the basic essay-format song and dance as well as a little grammar-exercise shuffle. I was going over how to do a first paragraph when the young man in the front row, who had rudely contradicted me earlier about the book for the class, raised his hand.

"Yes?" I said.

"Are you in the FBI?"

"No, I'm not," I said. Even though it seemed a bit strange, I decided to keep on lecturing. Obviously, I had some sort of delayed reaction and when it finally dawned on me what he had said, I asked, "Why do you think I'm in the FBI?"

"Because you have that look. And you're wearing brown shoes," he said with a confirming nod. "FBI agents like brown shoes." There was not another sound in that class of 33. No fidgeting, nothing.

"What if I had worn black shoes?" I asked.

"That's CIA."

"Oh. Do you have much experience with the FBI?"

"Sure. They watch me a lot."

"Why?"

"Because they think I can perform minor miracles."

Minor miracles. I looked at this brown headed, pudgy, accountant looking man and couldn't help but ask, "Can you?"

"Of course," he replied as if I'd asked if the sky were blue.

"What kind of miracles?" I asked with my penchant for prodding a bit too much.

"Any kind. Remember the rainbow around the moon last Saturday night?"

"No," I said, "I don't."

One of the other students volunteered, "There was a huge thunderstorm last Saturday night."

"Okay. So after the thunderstorm, there was a rainbow around the moon?" I repeated slowly for clarification.

"Yes," he said, "I put it there." He shrugged. "I do stuff like that all time. But first I have to drink 4 bottles of Vicks Formula 44D cough syrup." Wow. If only I'd known miracles were that easy.

I saw the Director of Night Studies in the hall. I had been told he walked around on the first night of class to help out if there were any problems; I think this one counted. I told the students to get started on their assignment, and I walked out and found him.

"I have a crazy guy in my class." I love to mince words.

"What?" he asked. So I told him what had happened and he added, "Well, he doesn't sound violent. Talk to him some more and see if maybe he was just joking. Don't worry! We will always have your back." With that, he patted me on my back in a *very* friendly fashion and left. I went back to the classroom and told the students that they could leave as soon as they turned in their paragraphs.

When Moon Man turned his in, I attempted friendly conversation and asked nonchalantly, "So, what do you do?"

"I started a job waiting tables at The Catfish Hut day before yesterday, but I'm gonna have to quit."

"Why?"

"I just found out I'm circumcised and can't do any heavy lifting," he said, shaking his head sadly. And he walked out. He wasn't in class on Thursday. I found out later that he had been asked to leave school Wednesday after he sat on the sidewalk outside the main campus building in a lotus position all day with a phone book on his head. I felt genuinely sorry for a guy who at the age of thirty had just realized he was circumcised; it had been one of my earliest and most pleasurable discoveries.

6

One of my favorite things in the world to do at the big old house was sit on the front porch in the swing as the sun was setting. I loved that big old swing and the comforting, steady "creak, creak" sound it made as I sat there and swung, safe for a few moments while the world sauntered by. No matter what kind of day I'd had, just sitting there somehow made it all better.

As the sun was setting, it was almost possible to overlook the semi-run down neighborhood or the silent, subtle desperation in the lives and actions of the people on the sidewalks and streets. This neighborhood used to be so different. When I was growing up, I rode my bike all over the place; sometimes not coming home until way after dark, and the only concern Mamma had was that I'd missed dinner. I was never afraid. We knew everybody. Not anymore. Both Trisha's and Caleb's bikes had been stolen within the last month. The other night I swear I heard gunshots. And I'd seen (for want of a better word) gangs of kids ranging in age from about fourteen and sixteen all the way down to four or five – too young to be out that late- roaming the streets at all hours even on school nights. It's very difficult to see a place you love disintegrate before your eyes. People didn't seem to care about this neighborhood anymore. Grass needed cutting; there was palpable decay that infected everything.

But sitting here on the porch at dusk, I could forget all of that. Occasionally, the kids would come out and keep me company. This particular evening was a little cool, not too bad, just enough of a nip in the air to need a sleeve but not enough for a jacket. Allie looked out the big oval glass in the front door and then came out and got on the swing with me. She skootched close to me and took my arm and crossed it over her body, protecting her face from the slightly chilled air. All I could see were her big brown eyes, the only brown eyed one of the bunch. Sometimes I thought that was all she was because she was so skinny.

We sat there, swinging slowly back and forth, watching the day get darker and darker. Just on the edge of darkness, I saw a lone figure making its way up the street. As the figure got closer, I saw that it was a man, slightly built, with long curly brown hair, dressed in dirty jeans and a stained, torn t-shirt. He was holding something in a brown paper bag and was making his way past our house to the seedy trailer park about eight blocks down our street. I knew the place pretty well because that was where Lynn had been hanging her hat lately, not so much to be close to the kids as to be close to the food grandparents, and sometimes we, provided. I watched him as he made his way up the street. A few houses down, he looked up, saw us, and crossed to the far side of the road, as far as he could away from our house and us and continued his trek. He walked past the house, not looking up from his feet at all. Allie and I watched him continue until he was lost in the darkness.

Allie shifted on the swing a little and said in a voice that was almost a whisper, "That was my daddy."

"Yeah, baby, it was," I said, pulling her closer and squeezing her to me, her need overpowering my discomfort; I'd recognized him a few minutes before. There was nothing else to say.

"Come on. It's getting cold. Let's go inside and see what Mammaw cooked for dinner."

The next time we saw her daddy, he was handcuffed and in a police car. He had tried to kill Lynn. Pushed her head through her bathroom window and kicked her a few times with his steel-toed boots because they were drunk and arguing and Lynn called him a "fucking faggot with a little dick" that he "didn't know how to use." That was after midnight. How she made it to our house, I'll never know. There was a trail of blood on the steps out front, on the front porch, on the glass in the front door, and in the hall. All I remember is Mamma's frantic yell.

She had heard Lynn fall against the door and was the first to see her. I got downstairs to find her on the floor, blood everywhere. Mamma was next to her, holding a shirt she'd picked up off the floor on Lynn's nose. Allie was standing in the bedroom door, quiet now; I had heard her screaming "Mamma" as I came down the stairs. Caleb was real quiet too, but I could see he was crying. The counselor said this led directly to the panic attacks Allie would have years later and the anger management issues that Caleb would face. I told them to go back to bed and me or Mamma would come in in a minute.

Lynn wasn't feeling anything. The ambulance came, but she wouldn't go with them. She just sat in the floor for a while; that was when we saw the police car drive by – the ambulance had reported Allie's dad. Lynn slept on our couch, Caleb and Allie refusing to leave her side; she went home the next morning, refusing to press charges because, as she said, "she really had to learn to keep her mouth shut."

7

"Look at 'em. Just a generation out of the trees."

I had been sitting on a bench outside the main administrative building enjoying the day and watching a group of young black men being young when my *learned* colleague came up beside me and uttered his words of wisdom. I looked over at him and didn't say anything; how does one handle racism that is no longer overt but instead bubbles underneath the surface? I continued to look at this professed Christian, feeling sorry for him, knowing that no matter how much education a person has there are some things that can not be unlearned. After a few minutes of prolonged heavy past-encrusted silence, he became embarrassed. His face colored and he left with a hastily muttered, "Talk to you later." I watched him go and then returned my attention to the young people just being young as only those not weighed down by life can be. Yes, it was a beautiful day.

Not too long after that, I found the Black Student Association; it was being run by a very nice black woman from the Workforce Development area of the college. When I went by her office and told her that Dr. Ryan had strongly suggested I come by and offer my services, she said, "You too?" Then she said, "I took over last fall; we've already decided to change the name to Multicultural Student Association and I've listed you as my co-advisor." Darn. I was looking forward to being an advisor to the Black Student Association; I'd already told a few of my co-workers just to see their momentary look of confusion.

I realize I am not cool; I have never been cool. In fact, I would

31

probably hurt myself if I made any attempt to be cool, but there was this very tiny glimmer in a small part of my brain who would love to walk down the halls wearing super sagging pants, a bandana, and a smart gold grille gleaming from my upper teeth. Students would part ways and give me the "Whas up?" sign. Sigh.

"What do I do first?" I asked, not having a clue about any student organization, either black or multicultural.

"Well, we're having a dance next Thursday night as our major fundraiser of the year. We need a DJ, approval to use campus facilities, extra security, a money box, and to put up fliers advertising the dance everywhere on campus. Which do you want?"

"I'll get the money box," I said, smiling.

She laughed, a good hearty laugh, then she gave me half the list.

We called the dance the Melting Pot Mixer; hoping it would establish us in the hearts and minds of the student body. The DJs were these two guys named AllThat and Mr. Z. At some point in the evening, they started calling me G Train because they said it gave me street cred. It was a party. The fliers had said to come and get "crunk" and that things would be "unhooked" or maybe that was "off the hook"; I usually get lost in modern slang, but I must admit that I was dizzy with the power of my street cred. There was only one student who trailed bong residue, and he was politely asked to leave by the two beefy security guards on stand by. I got to listen to some classic songs like "Shake Your Tail Feathers," "Get Low," and my personal favorite "Like a Pimp," the remix, not the original. And the dancing! There were students on the dance floor who were obviously checking each other for lice. In fact, I felt quite certain that nine months from that night we would see some Melting Pot Mixer babies. The dance was a great success; more people attended than had at any other school-sponsored event. And I like to think my cool quotient went way up. I wonder how much grilles cost.

8

Even though I had started teaching full time, money was still an issue at home. Because I didn't have any and the neighborhood was becoming even more strange. That's not really right. It was becoming dangerous. First, my ex-stepfather, Les, moved in nearby. This is my sisters' father. My father died when I was two, and my mother remarried when I was four; I guess Les was the only father I'd ever known. God, what a thought! That man never wanted me; he tried to get Mamma to give me to my father's relatives before they got married. She refused but married him anyway because she was pregnant with Lynn, thus beginning my scenic route through Hell.

He was so wonderful and thoughtful in public; people would say how lucky I was to have such a good step dad. Bullshit. He was a vindictive, cruel, petty nothing of a man who took every opportunity to belittle my mother or his other favorite target, me. Once, Mamma and I got back from a weekend trip to the coast to visit my father's mother and found that Les had donated all of our clothes to the Salvation Army. Mamma had to borrow clothes to go to work in.

His favorite place to punish me was the laundry room. It was always so dark and dank, and I never understood exactly what I'd done. I gave him some look or used a tone of voice. And he'd lock me in. It was scary at first at least until I learned not to react. Total equilibrium. To this day, whenever I feel the world is against me, I sit in the laundry room. That's where I learned to find my balance. I could empty myself out there so that I wouldn't feel anything. You can't get hurt or scared or ashamed if you don't feel.

There is something else. Something I've never told anyone: One day, not long after they got married, Mamma ran somewhere, maybe the grocery store or the bank. After she drove off, he called me. I walked down the hallway and saw him in the bathroom. Naked. Wrapped in a towel. He just stared at me; then he picked me up and stood me on the toilet. I didn't say anything. He didn't like for me to talk at all; I was always afraid that I would somehow use "that tone" that made him so mad. He unbuttoned my pants and slid them down to the cowboy boots I had gotten last Christmas. He felt my legs, all the way up. With a hand on either side of my hip, he pulled my underwear down, letting them come to rest on my pants. With his right hand, he felt my penis; first cupping it in his hand then rubbing it between his thumb and forefinger.

He almost-whispered, "You'll have a nice one, one day, Sweet Baby." Everything else was so quiet, waiting. Like it didn't know what to feel or how to feel either. The slight drip of the faucet. The rustle of the shower curtain from a breeze coming through the open window. He looked at my eyes. He always said I had beautiful eyes. I looked at his eyes. They were dark with thick brows and lashes. There was nothing there. He hated me. He went down on his knees and leaned in, taking all of my penis in his mouth. I shifted back because he had a day's growth of beard; he put his left hand on my behind and pushed me forward and deeper into his mouth which was almost too hot. He removed the towel, reached up with his right hand and got three squirts of the Jergens lotion sitting there on the vanity and started masturbating. I just stood there.

The light wasn't on, but I could see dead bugs in the fixture overhead. The medicine cabinet on the wall was open just enough for me to see my face. There was half a bottle of shampoo on the edge of the tub next to the washcloth I had used the night before. There I was again, in the mirror; it was smudged in the lower right corner. I scrunched my face as I felt him suck harder, wincing as he used his teeth. There was a tingling in my stomach, an almost pleasure, a growing knot of … something, leaking tendrils of not-fulfillment, confusion, and a lot of guilt. He started moaning softly and let out one loud grunt followed by heavy gulps of air. Something had flown out of his penis and onto the wall behind the toilet; a haphazard stream of white on the pale blue that my mother had painted a few months earlier.

He sat back on the balls of his feet, freeing my penis from his mouth. He stood up, wrapping the towel back around his waist, and grabbed the washcloth, wiping his trail off the wall. Then he turned and left, whistling as he walked down the hall. I pulled up my underwear and my pants, got down from the toilet and used a piece of tissue to wipe off the three white drops I saw on my boots. I opened the lid, threw the paper in the water and stood there watching the paper swirl around the bowl and then disappear.

He did that whenever Mamma went somewhere. Every time.

Hell lasted a total of five years. They were together maybe three years altogether. They'd fight; we'd go to my grandparents; then, we'd go back. They'd fight; we'd go to one of Mamma's friends; then, we'd go back. Somewhere in there, Mamma had Lynn and Sara. And then they finally divorced. After he took the sleeping pills. In grandma's living room. He had called saying that he wanted to "see his children" then he came over and tried to talk to Mamma and convince her to come back to him. They sat in the living room for a long time having a whispered argument. I was in the bedroom sitting next to the door, trying to listen. Mamma said later that Les pulled out a bottle of pills, put them on the coffee table and said, "If you don't come back to me, I have nothing to live for." Mamma called my name and I just knew we'd be going with him, but when I got in the living room, Mamma said, "Go get him a glass of water." Les looked really surprised and I ran to the kitchen and got the big plastic glass that grandma used to water the dog, filled it and took it to the living room and put it on the coffee table, right next to the pill bottle. I stood next to Mamma's chair; she'd put her arm around me. We watched Les sitting on the couch. He finally picked up the pills, opened the child-safety top and poured them in his mouth. Then he picked up the water and drank. He put the glass down and looked at my mother. She didn't say anything. I didn't say anything. After a time, Les started to fidget. He said, "Ain't you gonna do anything?" and Mamma said, "Why? I got insurance on you." Les grabbed the pill bottle and ran out the door. We heard that he made it to the hospital, and they had to pump his stomach. Mamma and Les divorced soon after that.

I wasn't happy when he moved into our neighborhood. As I said, he wasn't any kind of step-father. But, to be honest, he really was an excellent grandfather; the kids adored him. A couple of years after he divorced my mother, which Mamma still refers to as the "happiest day of my life," he came out of the closet and became the drag queen More-or-Les. Mamma said that now he was getting exactly what he deserved exactly where he deserved it. She was somehow able to come to terms with him and reach an alliance of sorts. I couldn't. All I could think was that he'd done nothing but hurt us and here he was next door and the kids liked him better than me. He was the Pied Piper; he played anything the kids wanted, and when I wasn't working, I lurked, watching, making sure that he was never alone with any of them. Mamma and the older kids thought I was manic. He knew, and I guess accepted it as the price of coming back into our lives.

About a month after they'd moved in, Mamma had taken Caleb, Allie, and Diane down to see their mother, and Trisha and Megan were helping my grandmother across the street. I was sitting in the swing on the front porch drinking a cup of coffee, and I saw Les making his way slowly up the sidewalk to our house. He used to be such a handsome man; everyone said so. There was barely an echo left of his formerly thick, dark hair, and he let one small piece grow to his shoulder and twirled it over the top of his head using lots of hair spray to keep it down. He had ballooned up to over three hundred pounds due to his drinking and, we later learned, Hepatitis C. His legs were always swollen and his feet had an unhealthy purplish tint to them. He wore flip flops, jogging pants, and extra extra extra large t-shirts. His belly was so swollen that his belly button had been inverted and poked out. None of this stopped his drinking. He and Jay, his lover of fifteen years, loved their vodka, usually mixed with Crystal Light. He made his way up to the house, struggling up the three stairs in the yard and the stoop to the porch. He stopped to catch his breath.

"Hey," he said breathlessly, leaning against the rail, his face red from the exertion.

"No one's here," I said, pushing the words out, not wanting him to invade my peace.

"Damn," he finished climbing the stairs and looked through the glass in the front door. "I told the kids I'd make them pancakes."

"They'll be back in a little while."

"I guess I'll come back and do the dew then," he said with a little jig. He turned to walk away then he stopped and turned back "You okay?"

"Sure."

"Even with me moving in?"

"No," my Southern gentility evaporating; I could see the smoky wisps of that gentility float away and curl through the tree next to the porch, "I'm not okay with that."

"I didn't think so," he hobbled back over to the swing and sat down; the screws in the ceiling holding the chain to the swing actually looked as if they were in pain. I hoped they stayed in there.

"The kids need me. Your Mamma needs me. I can be a help. I need to be a help."

"Maybe," I couldn't look at his face. "You sick bastard; you have no right to be here."

His voice got low and lost the high pitch he usually affected. "I wasn't good to you. It's like I got this chain around these ol' useless legs always pestering me. How can I undo something that was done by someone who was not me?" he asked trying to straighten out his legs. The heels were cracked and very dry; they'd been bleeding recently.

"Bull shit. Who was it then? Why are you here?"

"Everyone deserves a second chance."

"No. They don't."

He put his hand on my knee, friendly like at first, but that bloated hand started caressing me.

"Don't touch me," I said. I looked down at his hand on my inner thigh, feeling those hard forgotten tendrils start in my groin. How could I start getting excited over this piece of nothing?

He said, "How I must have hurt you, my Sweet Baby." The heart is a four-chambered organ, two ventricles and two atriums; my ventricles froze, my atriums withered.

"Get your fucking hand off of me," I said, tonelessly, trying to keep all emotion out of my voice though I could feel my face getting red. "And don't call me that, ever."

"You never told your Mamma. Why not?"

"Because it would have destroyed her. It still would. So I just try to pretend that it didn't happen. That works, mostly."

He grabbed the swing chain with one hand and ran his other hand through the still thick hair on the sides of his head. "So much of my life was spent being screwed up. I was forced to be something I wasn't. I got married and tried to change, to be someone else, and that made me into someone I hated." He stopped and looked out at the yard filled with children's toys strewn everywhere. "Maybe I could pretend it didn't happen too."

"I won't let you do that. It's not right. I will tolerate you because the kids and Mamma love you. But I do hate you." I looked at his hands clasped saint-like in his lap then I looked at my hands. Ragged fingernails that never got the chance to grow before they were bitten off. "I don't want to know your reasons. They don't matter. We make ourselves. I got to believe that. And if you think you're the only one screwed up, try living in my head."

"I love those kids." I saw Mamma's minivan coming down the road. She beeped when she saw us.

"I know. I do too."

"Nothing will ever happen to them. I promise. I'm not that person anymore." Mamma pulled into the carport. Caleb and Ashley struggled to unbuckle and get out. Mamma helped Diane out of the car seat.

"If you do," I said, matter-of-factly, looking at his dark brows and lashes, "I will blow your god damned head off." I looked down again. "You know I already want to."

He smiled sadly and said, "I know. You're my inoculation."

The kids ran up and hugged Les' legs. He said, "Who wants pancakes?" and struggled to his feet; he went to the door that Mamma had just opened and taken Diane through. The others had hurtled through as soon as they heard "pancakes." He stopped at the threshold and said without turning around, "How you must hate me."

"Wouldn't you hate you?"

"Yes, more than anything." And he walked inside.

"I don't hate you. I should, but I can't find that feeling." I watched that pathetic shadow of a man walk down the hall to the kitchen and continued talking as if he were still standing there, "Hating you would give you some kind of power over me. It isn't necessary to hate you." I sat there in silence for a few moments, listening to the kids yelling and Les laughing and Mamma too. I drank the last bit of coffee in my cup; it was cold and the bitter aftertaste refused to go away. I looked up and saw my mother at the door. She smiled warmly and said, "Les wants to know if you want any pancakes."

9

Dr. Dennis came by my office, stuck her head in the doorway and said, "Are you busy?"

"No," I replied, "What's up?" I always felt comfortable around her.

"Nothing, really," she said in her breathless manner. She came in the office and closed the door. "I don't want just anyone to hear what I have to say."

"Okay."

"First and most important, I want you to know that what you are is important to me. I don't care about anything except you being a good teacher."

"Okay," I said again, even more slowly, not having a clue what this conversation was about or where it was going.

"What I'm saying is that I know you're gay. I've always known."

"Oh," I said with a sinking feeling. I know this was supposed to be a place of higher learning with lots of educated people, but it is still Mississippi and Baptist to boot. "How did you know?" I knew I wasn't the most masculine guy, but I didn't think I was putting out any vibes.

"I've known for years. You once wore a head band to my class. I just loved the eighties, didn't you?" She looked over at me. "Don't you worry about a thing, dear," she said, "I said I don't care where you put what; I just have a question to ask." She pulled a picture out of her dress pocket, put it on the desk and slid it over to me. In it was a

40

very handsome brown haired man, about thirty, with what appeared to be an easy going smile. "This is my son-in-law, Kenneth. He and my daughter are divorcing," then she dropped her voice to a stage whisper, "He's gay too." I was still clueless about what she needed, so I just silently nodded my head and gave her a stiff smile. She looked up at me expectantly and said, "Do you know him?"

"No," I said.

"Are you sure? Come on. There can't be that many gay guys around here. Maybe you've seen him out or at one of those parties I'm always hearing about."

"What parties?"

"The ones where everyone gets naked and has their way with everybody else. The one that Zelda Crimshy caught her husband getting screwed by that black highway patrol officer and sued him for everything he was worth."

I knew about Howard Crimshy, everyone did; it went through this town fast, as only good gossip can. He was a pathetic man who had lost his house and his kids and had moved to Jackson and gotten a job as a nurse at the Medical Center. He was undergoing religious therapy to change his orientation. He would go to therapy every Tuesday and Thursday evening and cruise the parks as soon as his therapy sessions were over. I used to think he was handsome; now, I'm told he looks haggard and he never looks anyone in the eyes and he just won't talk. "It wasn't a party; he just invited the guy over and his wife came home to surprise him. She ended up being the one getting the surprise."

"There are the other parties. The one with the mayor and that guy who owns the men's wear store. And that urologist, and that guy who owns the horse arena."

I'd heard the same stories. Zelda had claimed to have a video of her husband with the highway patrolman; then the story just ballooned. Before too long, any questionable male in the area was now going to a monthly poker party that, according to "reliable" sources, quickly became an orgy. Zelda later confessed to a good friend of mine that there had never been a video; she'd just said that to make "that little bastard" she'd been married to sweat.

"Don't believe any of those stories," I said.

"Why not? How do you know they're not true?" she asked.

"Because I haven't been invited to not one of the orgies. And I would have been. You know gay men have great taste." I looked at the poster on my wall; I knew if I looked at her I'd laugh.

She looked at me for a minute, started laughing, then coughed demurely and said, "I guess you're right."

"And Dr. Dennis, I don't have a listing of gay guys in the area. I really wish I did. There isn't even a secret handshake that I know about."

"How do you meet anyone?"

"I don't."

"Why not?"

"The kids. You know how it is; my cup runneth over. And there's no extra money for dating. Plus where would I take them if I had someone, the storage shed outside my house?" I laughed a bit, "I can just see it now; I meet a cute guy and take him home and then say, 'See that building down the hill; meet me there. I'll get down there as soon as I can get the kids to bed.'"

"That would ruin the romance," she agreed; then, she reached over the desk and patted my hand. "It'll be okay. You'll meet someone. In the mean time, if you see Kenneth out anywhere, let me know." And she got up to leave.

"Sure," I said, "But you could save us both some trouble and introduce me to your son-in-law."

"I'm not quite that open minded." She opened the door to my office and, as she stepped from the carpet on my office floor to the tile in the hallway, her foot slipped out from under her. She managed to barely catch herself on the side of the doorway. "I could have fallen on my butt!" she said indignantly. Then she turned back to me and whispered, "And me not wearing any underwear!" She brushed her skirt. "There I'd be, just flashing my poon poon for the world to see. Talk to you later, dear."

10

Les still did drag every once in a while at the local gay club, a desolate little place that used to be a gas station. It was just off of the interstate, about eight miles from town. It was also the area dump; you pass six large dumpsters before you can park and go in. There couldn't be a better illustration for being gay in Mississippi. But it was the only place for us to meet for a couple of hundred miles; I would go occasionally when the need becomes too powerful to ignore, and I could scrape together the five dollars necessary to get in. I didn't like to go too often for two very specific reasons.

First, if Les was there, he would always yell, "There's my son!" and "That's my boy!" as loudly as he possibly could, and I didn't want anyone in the universe thinking that I was related to him. I would be forced to spend the rest of the evening trying to explain that while I did know that deluded man who loved to wear mascara, we were not in any way related.

Second, I would always run into students, both present and former, or colleagues who would try to hide or act embarrassed to be seen there. I always went up to them, made eye contact, and spoke. I would never bring the subject up at school because I didn't feel it was appropriate, but I did want them to know that I wasn't embarrassed. Of course, at work, I was typically in major stealth mode, trying not to show up on anyone's radar too much.

Les now focused more on comedy and usually put on interesting shows; for his last show last Christmas, he put antlers on a goat and put it on stage – it peed while he was doing his signature Tina Turner song, "Rolling On The River." The crowd went wild.

Les and Jay weren't the only additions to the neighborhood. A crack house opened three houses down from us, right behind the Baptist church. At first, I couldn't say with one hundred percent certainty that it was a crack house. I can say that the people who went in and came out of it all day and night looked and acted a bit peculiar. And one of the guys who owned or rented or stayed there free came by the house one night when I was sitting in the swing on the porch and offered to sell me "something that would make my toes curl." Now I'm all for toe curling in any non-pharmaceutical manner. It didn't help that the crack house was frequented by my sister Sara's husband Kurt who had so many addictions we actually lost count. Or that he owed them money. We found out that he owed them money when a young black man came by our house and told us. He asked for Sara and told her that Kurt owed him $200 and if he (or she) didn't pay that "he might come by and shoot through the walls."

Sara went across the street to Les. He was getting ready for a show and had his nails, the all purpose duct tape, pantyhose and heels on with another panty hose on his head holding down his hair. That was all. His upper body (with his man breasts) was bare because the dress and wig are always the last to go on. When Sara told him what the guy said, he didn't stop to change or put any more clothes on. He picked up a baseball bat, got in her car and had her drive him to the crack house.

My ex-stepfather went into that house, found two young men, pulled himself up to his full 6 foot 2 inch, former Marine height and his 300 hundred pound post Marine weight, pointed the bat in the chest of the man who had just been to our house and bellowed, "I don't know who the hell you think you are but those are my grandkids in that house and I will kill yo' ass if you ever go near them again." He raised the baseball bat for emphasis. "And when I do kill you, I'll shove this bat so far up your ass, your throat will get splinters." Sara said the two men just sat there on a raggedy couch, unable to talk. Les snorted loudly and took the pantyhose off of his head, threw it at them and left, muttering to himself. He used to scare me as a child, but damn it felt good to have that particular half-dressed, deranged drag queen on our side.

That was the last straw for Sara; she divorced Kurt. And got full custody of their daughter Mckenna, mainly because Kurt was in jail due to his bad tendency to get DUI's. Those alleged drug dealers probably had never seen someone of that caliber before; they didn't bother us again. Two days later there was some sort of shoot out over there. I guess someone didn't like the way their toes got curled or some such.

The Neighborhood Watch meeting that month was filled to overflowing. A policeman came to talk to us about safety and explain why, even though the police knew it "fit the crack house profile" and many illicit things were being sold there, nothing could be done; the explanation – in my opinion - boiled down to "we're afraid of getting shot." They should have enlisted Les' help. In fact, he was there and offered, but they declined. About the only thing decided that night was that we needed Children-At-Play signs so that cars would slow down as they went through the area.

To pay for the signs, we decided to have a cookout and garage sale. We were able to use the parking lot of the Baptist Church which was just in front of the crack house, and we grilled chicken and burgers. The nosey older woman who lived just down from us provided a lot of the chicken. I bought a plate and sat down next to her at one of the tables. I took a bite of the chicken and decided quickly to stick to the watery potato salad. Even the bread looked suspect. Nosey neighbor walked up to me and said in a friendly way, "How do you like my chicken?"

"It's good," I lied.

"It's a family recipe. I soak it in Coca Cola before putting it on the grill."

"Maybe I should write this down," I said nodding my head encouragingly, even though I was really thinking about shouting a warning to everybody, "because that sure is unusual." A few minutes later, I saw Mamma and said, "We really got to get out of this neighborhood."

11

"Mr. Stewart?" the barely eighteen year old girl standing at my front door said, smiling shyly, looking very fragile and about to break.

"Sandy, what are you doing here?" I kind of demanded, not opening the door completely and feeling very self conscious in the shorts and t-shirt I was wearing. Not my most professional. My stomach fell through the soles of my feet and puddled on the floor.

"I just wanted to see you."

"Sandy, you don't come to my home. Ever. Do you understand? How did you find it anyway?"

"You said you live in this neighborhood, so I just drove up and down the streets until I found your car." Stalking 101. Not part of most liberal arts education.

This was what happens sometimes when a teacher is nice to a student (or even when a teacher isn't nice to a student). Especially if the student is needy and immature. Sometimes the student misinterprets the attention and concern and thinks it's something else. This student definitely misinterpreted something – I was not sure exactly what. I was very nice to her at first, but she started getting moon eyed, stopping by my office a lot; I made sure the door was open at all times and that there was a lot of traffic in the hall outside. She would just sit until I had to tell her to leave, and she got to be a little too touchy for my taste, making sure she accidentally brushed the back of my hand or my shoulder. Then she gave me a note after class one day that read:

Mr. Stewart

> *Hey, I really needed to talk to you about something, but you weren't in your office. Maybe I'll talk to you Monday. Remember yesterday when you ask me if something was wrong and I said no. Well there is. I don't really want to talk to you about my problem or I would say situation, but I need you to know, because you're part of it. But I am afraid that you don't want to hear it, but I hope so. I don't really want to say it in a letter but if I have to I will. I just know it is driving me crazy. Also, Paige thinks your kind of funny because your not married, but I hope not. Well I need to go. So I'll talk to you later.*

Sandy

I had to put up some definite boundaries and stick to them. The problem was that I truly felt sorry for her. She was very socially inept; her sister Paige was in the class with her, and Sandy got lost in any comparison. Her sister was prettier by far and had an inner light that shined. I had tried to be nice to Sandy, and here she was on my doorstep.

"Mr. Stewart, I had an accident," she said, even though she seemed calm and looked okay, so did her car (which I could see over her shoulder parked in my driveway).

"When?"

"This morning." The sun was going down. It had to be close to 7 p.m. She obviously had an emergency going on here.

"Then you need to go home and tell your parents," and I closed the door and walked back to the kitchen. I sat at the table for at least fifteen minutes until I heard her car start and pull out of the driveway. I was furious.

There's that old saying "Don't shit where you eat." I didn't. I knew that there were professors who did fool around with students, but I felt that it was unethical. I know that this was college and everyone was supposed to be an adult but still. It would almost be like messing around with your psychiatrist. But if I were completely honest, it helped me maintain my intestinal fortitude and moral determination that no really good looking students had ever shown the slightest interest in me. At least I don't think so; I'm not good at noticing things like that. So easy to maintain moral fortitude when it isn't seriously challenged.

The next day in class, Sandy sat in her same seat next to her sister and seemed very subdued. At the end of class, I asked her to stay for a moment. Then I said, "You know what you did was unacceptable. You can't do that again. Understand?"

"Yes," she said in a quiet voice, looking like she might cry.

"I am your teacher and your friend, but that's it." Then I softened my voice and continued. "You're going to find friends your age, and I promise everything will be okay." I wanted to put my hand on her shoulder, but I knew I couldn't. Not now. I smiled at her instead. "Go home, Sandy. Just go home. Okay?"

She just nodded her head and left. I decided that I had better let someone higher up the food chain (in administration) know about everything in case there was ever a problem ("And the Lord said thou shalt cover thine butt"). I asked for and got an appointment with the Dean of Student Services, who used to be the Director of Night Studies, gave him the note and told him about Sandy's visit. He looked at it solemnly for a minute or two and then said,

"From what you've said, she's just a child. It's a crush, nothing more. I wouldn't worry too much about it. She'll be hurt a little, but she'll get over it. You did the right thing."

"That's what I thought, but I wanted someone else to be made aware of it just in case."

"If I were you, I'd be more concerned about the last part of the note. She thinks you might be 'funny.'" His right hand massaged his left and came to rest on his wedding band which he moved back and forth as if to scratch an itch underneath.

"As you said, she's just immature," I said, brushing it off and not wanting to venture into this topic at all with him. In one of my classes, a girl in the very back of a packed room raised her hand and asked, "Are you funny?" I answered, "I'm hysterical." And nothing else was ever said. Stealth mode.

"Well, if it doesn't bother you ..." he left that hanging, then he looked at me appraisingly and said, "You look like you've been working out."

"Trying to."

"Where do you go?"

"At home. I have some weights and a Bowflex. I thought I should try to get back into shape and knew I couldn't afford to join a gym with my *vast* fortune then I remembered the Bowflex in the corner of my room with clothes hanging all over it." I laughed a little. "I got it when I worked in Saudi, and it's been collecting dust ever since."

"Saudi?" and he looked at me again, "Arabia? You were there?"

"Yeah," I said. "Until I gave it all up for Mississippi."

"You sound like you miss it."

"It was a different time. There was money. And no responsibilities. Or at least not many." My laugh was forced and nervous.

"Well, you know what they say, 'Pride comes before the fall,'" he said, nodding his head as if he'd just let me in on the secret of the universe.

I just looked at him because I couldn't think of anything to say to that.

He continued, "You really should get out of your house and exercise in a gym. It's great. But find one with a sauna." He leaned back in his chair, clasped his hands behind his head, lost in thought and sighed, "That's the best part. There's nothing quite like sitting around with other men completely naked and without a care in the world. You should come some time as my guest. Just let me know."

"I'm really busy right now."

"Just let me know," he repeated, smiling broadly.

"I will." I stood up; he did too.

"And if you have any more trouble out of that student or you just want to talk …" he let the last statement fade away, his eyes drifting down to settle on my crotch. I nodded my head, and he reached out and shook my hand, squeezing it in a *very* friendly manner. I left a little hurriedly.

12

Sometimes Lynn called and wanted rides. The calls came from various pay phones and were always collect.

"Hello?"

"Hey, is Mamma there?" she always asked because any sympathy I had for her had been slowly leaking out for years. I handed the phone to Mamma who was sitting on the couch with her feet up because she had hurt her back the day before.

"What?" Mamma asked, putting the receiver to her ear, then she sighed and said, "I guess so. Be there in a minute." She hung up the phone and started trying to get to her feet.

"Mamma," I said, "you can't drive. You can barely walk."

"I told her I was coming," she said, struggling to her feet but unable to completely straighten up.

"I'll go," I said, trying to control my rage, "Where is she?"

"At the La Parisienne Motel," she said, sitting back down.

The La Parisienne Motel (and bar) had once been a great place to party. Almost 30 years ago. But it had not managed to keep up with the various city annexations and the new interstate highway system. Its once central location was now peripheral at best. It was an old, run down place with none of the European flavor its name suggested. Now it just needed paint, or a bulldozer. There were ladies walking up and down the street plying their trade. Seeing them made me wonder for the millionth time whether Lynn had ever done that. She hadn't worked in a long time. But she always had drugs and drink. Best not to think about that.

I pulled into the parking lot driving slowly to avoid the pot holes. There she was. God, she looked thin. But she'd done her make up and hair and looked relatively presentable in an I'm-going-out-to-a-bar-and-need-someone-to-buy-me-a-drink kind of way. She wouldn't have many years left to do that. She was in a sun dress that had seen better days and offered little protection from the chill in the air, and she bore bruises and scratches from somewhere although they had faded enough that make-up could cover them. And there was a man with her. A man about my height (six feet), thin, though not emaciated, more like a former athlete with salt and pepper hair and beard, the latter being quite formidable. Lynn opened the passenger side door, stuck her head in and said, "He's coming too, okay?" I didn't feel like arguing, so I didn't say anything, and they got in. Lynn on the passenger side and the Jesus look-alike in the back.

"Hey," he said, slurring slightly, and thrust his hand over the seat to shake. "I'm Steve but everybody calls me R.S. which stands for Reverend Steve which I used to be, but I'm not now on account of I lost my congregation."

"Oh. You're a preacher?" I asked although it was obvious he wasn't, or wasn't really a "practicing minister" judging by his somewhat altered state and the fact that he was going to screw my sister.

"No," and his voice cracked "And my life's just gotten worse and worse since then." He took out a pack of cigarettes, reached over the seat to give one to Lynn, lit hers, took one himself and lit it. He inhaled deeply and exhaled slowly, pensively. "But I think God only gives us what we can handle. He is the staff of comfort, so he's just trying to make us stronger. That's why he turned me to drink and other excesses. They was made by his holy hand, and he wouldn't a put this itch in me lessen he wanted me to scratch it. Sometimes the human spirit is just too weak to take on the power of the rapture but when I smoke that pipe and inhale those most holy vapors, I become the rapture and become a vessel for the Holy Ghost. And since I must share the spirit of the lord- he is the way, the power and the light- it's my duty to minister to these poor lost bastards. By indulging with them, I'm doing my part to bring them all back to Christ." All the time he was speaking he was fidgeting nervously and scratching at sores on his bare arms; stigmata of his very own personal crusade.

I pulled into the driveway of the trailer Lynn was staying at. There was cardboard covering the bathroom window.

Reverend Steve got out first. He came to my window and thrust his hand in. I shook it. Then he reached in and hugged me. He pulled back to arms length, put his palm on my forehead and looked up to heaven. Then he dropped his hand, stared wide-eyed into my face and said, "You want me to pray with you?"

"Not even a little," I said, trying for, but not quite finding, a tone that was slightly apologetic.

"You sure? It might get you extra points with …" and he pointed heavenward.

"You know what? I think I'm going to risk it," I said.

Lynn crawled out of the passenger seat and headed for the trailer. "Thanks," she said over her shoulder. She had left her purse on the front seat. I watched Lynn go to the door and push it open; it wasn't locked – what would be the point? She stood back and let Reverend Steve, the pied piper with a special pipe, go on in. I rolled down my window and yelled, "You forgot your purse." She made an I'll-be-there-in-a-minute gesture and followed the reverend in. I hurriedly reached in the console between the seats, pulled out three condoms (lubricated) that were in a box in there, trying not to think about how long it had been since I'd needed one, and a couple of non-lubricated ones (mint flavored) and threw them in her purse. Never put all of your faith in a religious man. She ran back to the car, grabbed her purse, thanked me again, and ran inside. I heard them laughing as I rolled the window up and pulled away. Reverend Steve. Smoking crack for Jesus.

13

In the late spring, years after my triumphant return to the states, we decided it was finally time to give up on our neighborhood. My mother sold her house, I sold my house, and we bought a three bedroom, two and a half bath house with a fireplace; all of this sat in the middle of five acres of forest that we were now responsible for. The house was at the end of a dirt road, at the top of a hill. You didn't come to our house unless you were visiting us or you were lost. In fact, its location is probably the only reason we got the house for the price we got it even though it was quite a bit above what we'd hoped to pay. We'd been looking for almost two years, trying to get something in this particular school district. Mamma had taken to driving around, up side roads, trying to find houses for sale; one house the realtor showed us was, as she said, "absolutely perfect for" us – and it was, five bedrooms, three and a half baths, $175,000 – but there was no way we could buy it and eat or pay utilities or drive, plus we would have had to have it financed through a company called Last Chance Mortgages.

Then one day Mamma saw a "for sale" sign that had fallen down. The house had been on the market for over a year and a half; no one had bothered to look at it. Because it was at the end of a dirt road at the top of a hill. Perfect. We settled in nicely.

Mamma got one bedroom, Trisha and Megan got one, and Allie and Diane got the last. Caleb and I got to sleep in the living room for the first seven months until we could enclose the carport; then he and I got to share a bedroom.

After we bought the house, it immediately began to fall apart. The first thing to go was the dishwasher; the only time it technically worked was during the last walk through before we bought the house. As soon as the papers were signed, that dishwasher threw in the towel.

And the toilet in the half bath had the bad tendency to bubble whenever someone took a shower in the middle bathroom. And the lights over the vanity in the last bathroom didn't work; the second day we were in the house, Trisha went into the bathroom and turned on the lights which lit up like a camera flashing. Then, nothing. Home sweet home.

Diane loved to run in and show me all of the bugs and plants she has discovered in our yard. Or they would just run around the yard doing kid things, like fighting. Diane might come in crying and holding her side. Allie would follow immediately to say that Diane had run into her foot while she (Allie) was doing karate. Allie didn't take karate; she just loved to kick things. It must have been the country air.

Trisha took to the new house and school nicely and even got a new boyfriend. Her boyfriend Will (or is it Wayne?) seemed pretty nice. She broke up with her old boyfriend a few months ago saying he was a dork. I didn't realize what this meant until I heard that that guy's new girlfriend was pregnant. Wayne (or maybe Wyatt) was eighteen, had dropped out of high school but was "working on" his GED, worked on a pipeline (or did before he got homesick and said the pipeline people weren't treating him right), and wasn't a dork. I didn't sleep at night.

Mamma didn't seem to let anything bother her. It was so damn frustrating. I ran around yelling and screaming and letting my blood pressure leap to unheard of heights while she just sat there, calm and cool, basking in the adoration of the children.

This is my mother: Diane's kindergarten class invited parents or grandparents or other surrogates to eat lunch with their kids in the school cafeteria. Mamma went as she had done with all of the kids. She said she couldn't be there when my sisters and I were young, but she was making up for it now. She and Diane got their trays, went through the lunch line together and sat down at one end of a long row of small tables. They set out their napkins and plastic spoons. One of Diane's friends came up and stood hesitantly by the table. Mamma looked at her, smiled, and said, "Hey. How are you?"

The girl just stood there and said, "My mamma and daddy couldn't come today. They really had to work." The girl was trying to smile, but her eyes were shining, almost making full tears.

"You sit down here," Mamma said, patting an empty chair next to her so she'd be between Diane and her friend, "Today, we'll pretend that I'm your grandma too." Before too long, there were kids all around her, calling her Mawmaw. They still do. She can't really be my mother.

I came home after my night class last Wednesday, and my fourteen year old Megan was sitting in a truck with a sixteen year old boy on the dirt road leading to our house. With a boy. In a truck. "Parking." My mind just could not wrap itself around the concept and, I must admit, I didn't handle it well. I did see that they were sitting on opposite sides of his truck, and everyone was enjoying the benefits of being fully clothed. This, however, didn't detract from the fact that he was supposed to be bringing her home from cheerleading practice. And that she was still just fourteen. The last was completely lost on her.

She came in the house crying and saying that I had embarrassed her - the boy having apparently run for the hills; then she said, "Why don't you trust me? I'm not my mother." Epiphanies suck. No, she was not Lynn who would have already bedded the poor child and been looking for a main course, probably one involving alcohol or some other mind altering substance which could be taken either in pill form or injected directly. I couldn't help comparing her to her mother because Megan was the one that looked the most like Lynn and, based on family history and demonstrated fertility, I was just not comfortable with the kids having sex. Ever. But that's not really fair, and I guess it would be nice if someone in the world were having sex. Megan was an Uber-Lynn who had never given me cause to doubt her. She was a Lynn with good teeth, posture and self esteem. A competitive cheerleader and a straight A student who planned to be a nurse. And was absolutely beautiful.

I needed a training manual—Parenting for Dummies which better have a chapter about girls who are just fourteen sitting in trucks with boys who might find themselves in a hole somewhere on five acres.

14

Caleb got to have the first party at the new house, a birthday party. He invited some friends to spend the night. It was cheaper than trying to go anywhere. Mamma made the cake. I got some pizzas, chips, cookies, and other sundries. Nothing extra for a gift. Just something else for me to feel guilty about. Five boys came ranging in age from ten to thirteen. My living room filled with pre-pubescent semi-angst ridden boys coated with sugar and caffeine so as not to upset the stomach. Tony, Mark, Jason, Ron. And David. I did not like David. Mr. Attitude. He kept watching me all night with a look that seemed to confirm that I was the stupidest person on the face of the earth. And I had to correct him a lot. Every time I turned around, he was underfoot.

"David, get off that – you'll get hurt."

"David, put that down – that's Allie's."

"David, don't touch Trisha's boob. That's not nice."

"No, David, I can't show you how to lift weights right now. Leave them alone."

"Get off the treadmill, you'll get hurt. Go play with the other boys, David." I sounded like a broken record. And that glare. They played football, then wrestled, then watched movies, ate sandwiches, wrestled again, got in bed by two, then joked, farted, belched, and cut up 'til 3:30. They got up at 7 a.m. and watched cartoons and ate cereal. "Okay ya'll; don't make a mess. David, pick up that cereal." God, I was tired. For every year the kids age, I age ten (dogs have dog years, parents have parent years, uncles have uncle years).

"David, that's my coffee cup – I use it everyday. I'll get you another glass." Glare. Lips pouting. Always watching. I couldn't stand that. He whispered to Caleb, and Caleb came over and whispered to me, "His name's not David; it's Sam. He was too embarrassed to tell you."

At noon the parents started picking up the kids. Thank god. I sat in a lawn chair in the front yard, tossing children to their parents with complete abandon. Caleb stood next to me. I put my arm around his shoulder.

"Did you have a good birthday?" I asked.

"Uh hunh."

"I can't believe how fast you're growing up. Soon you'll be driving." And my insurance rate will quadruple.

David (Sam) sat on the ground in front of us. Glaring. He was the last to leave. Everyone else had been gone at least half an hour. Then we heard this awful noise. A car I think. With no muffler or something else seriously wrong. I looked down the hill and saw a car turning down the dirt road to our house. A Nova. It was once blue, but the paint had peeled so much that its color depended completely on the lighting. The tires didn't look all that great, and the door couldn't be original. A worn looking woman was at the wheel with a cigarette dangling from the left side of her lip. I waved at her, but she acted like she didn't see me and didn't smile at all. Caleb later told me that Sam lived with his grandparents, and his mother didn't come around to see him a lot. He had an older brother and sister somewhere. Nothing was ever said about a dad.

"That's my mom," he said as he picked up a small, plastic grocery bag with his stuff. He then motioned Caleb over and whispered to him. Caleb looked up at me.

"Sam wants to know if he can hug you goodbye."

15

"Cat killed a goat," Mamma said, not too long after we had moved in. I was at work. Cat was our German Shepherd. We'd had him a little over a year. He followed Megan home one day and adopted us; I think he was afraid of the old neighborhood too and had heard we were leaving. She named him Cat because he "acted just like a cat." And Cat thought he was an inside dog which caused a constant struggle between me and the kids as I felt quite sure Cat would be more content on the outside.

"Why would he do that?" I asked Mamma, not knowing about any goats in our new area, but it was the country, and I suppose that they did have those types of domesticated things somewhere.

"I guess he's not used to being in the country," she said, "He's usually so gentle. And I told Mr. Jameson that too."

"Who's Mr. Jameson?"

"He owns the goat. He lives right down the road. I told him you'd come by after work to talk to him. Be nice. We don't want the reputation of being goat killers."

I turned off the engine, opened the car door, and got out. I was parked in front of a large, well kept trailer with three big fenced areas around it. A wooden deck had been built on the front of the trailer, and at the base of the stairs to the deck was a bloody mess. The door opened and an elderly man came out. He made his way down the stairs and met me about halfway between my car and the deck. He held out a calloused hand.

"Mr. Jameson," he said, introducing himself, grabbing my hand and squeezing very hard, "You must be Mr. Stewart."

"Hello," I replied, squeezing his hand back with equal pressure and then increasing the pressure just a bit, a real man handshake. I was also trying to find and put on my diplomat's hat to smooth over any ruffled neighbor feathers.

"There's the damage," he said, letting go of my hand and pointing to the mess. "He was one of my prized goats." This was accompanied with a forlorn shake of his head.

Great.

"I'm so sorry, Mr. Jameson," I said, feeling it. "Cat doesn't usually act like that. He's been around the children and never been mean at all."

"He probably never seen a goat before. I don't have any hurt feelings as long as you pay me what I'm out."

"How much is that, sir?"

"Eighty dollars," he said, looking down and shaking his head again, "That's what I could have sold him for."

"Right," I said, "I understand." I went back to my car, got my checkbook and wrote him a check. "We just moved in, and we really want to be good neighbors," I said as I handed him the check, hoping it wouldn't come back marked "Insufficient funds."

"Nothing's broken that can't be fixed," he said taking the check, folding it and putting it in his front pocket. He patted me hard on the back, "I raise the best goats in three counties, and you have just purchased the finest!" Then he chuckled and said, "Course, it's dead. But, hey, welcome to the neighborhood!"

16

My mother, the epitome of the "full figured" woman, had to go in to have her spine patched about every three months. She cracked it a year ago by lifting and turning in a way that she was not intended to, and it never healed properly. The pain, which she described as "slightly less than child birth," came and went, but definitely more of the former. This was in addition to the fibromyalgia and the degenerative arthritis. She had a lot of medication to take and, I believe, was in a lot of pain – more pain than she admitted to. It was there around her eyes and the set of her mouth. As a child, I remember her coming home from work (shooting rivets, cutting metal, lots of heavy lifting and pushing) and going to bed at 4 or 4:30pm. Absolutely exhausted. A single mom trying to provide for her kids. And she was paying dearly for it. She waited until late to take the bulk of her medication because she couldn't drive when she took it, and the kids might have needed her. She worried me; I watched her slowing down, her body unable to keep up. And I was so afraid of being left here by myself. I admired her attitude but hoped hers was not the road my body would take.

My family does not age well. We do okay until around thirty-five or forty. Then gravity and life start pulling us down. I guess for most people it would be difficult to suddenly not be able to be as active as they once were. And Mamma had always been active. She always had at least two jobs while my sisters and I were growing up. And, after the relative fiasco of her second marriage to Les, seemed perfectly content to be single. She said repeatedly, "I married for love twice; the first one died and the second one didn't want me because I didn't have a penis. I don't think I'll try it anymore."

She married my dad when she was sixteen – I always thought it was to get away from her parents, but she never admitted that. She had me when she was nineteen and was a widow by twenty-one; then came the marine with a taste for women's clothing. It would be a bit off putting for most people. She had been on a diet trying to lose a good bit of weight which seems to congregate in the general vicinity of her boobs and seems to be a family trait – the weight gain, not the weight gain around the boobs; I myself was known for the firmness of my chest. The doctor said she needed to lose weight. People who have weight issues just should not live in the South where everything is deep fried, including the salad. She had been very happy this morning because when she put on her pants, and they were loose. Then she saw that the elastic had broken.

Caleb got banned from the phone for the foreseeable future. He was mad because he said that we really didn't have a reason to ground him. And technically we didn't. But I thought he was too young to be discussing some of the things he was discussing: Trisha overheard one girl promise Caleb a blowjob the next time he went skating to prove her love for him. I couldn't deal with any more babies, and Caleb worried me more than Megan or any of the girls. I wanted to provide a firebreak for him. Caleb got mad and told me that he was "a man," and I just nodded my head; later that night he asked me if he could sleep with me because it was raining and thundering and lightening.

I was sitting on the couch, watching television when Diane came and sat next to me. We had watched together for a few minutes when she said, in an off handed manner, "I think I know what I want to do when I grow up."

"Really?" I said encouragingly. "What?"

"I want to wear a shiny, gold bikini and dance around a pole."

My heart started pounding so hard that I'm surprised she didn't look around wondering who was stomping through the house. I could have started shouting, saying how stupid that was and asking what she'd been watching on television because I thought the parental controls were on. I could have started denigrating exotic dancers, saying how dancing like that was bad for the ankles and that the lights make a person old before her time. I didn't say anything. I just sat there, not thinking at all about what was on television, hoping that she would forget this conversation. I was going to have to exercise more or I was going to have a heart attack.

We have had to curtail Allie's religious pursuits. She had started going to this church with her bus driver and the bus driver's family. They are wonderful people and have taken Allie into their hearts, saying that "there is just something special about that girl." Allie asked if she could be a cheerleader for the church, and I said that she could as long as her homework and studying weren't neglected. Then, they started practicing every evening. She didn't get home until about 8 or 8:30 p.m. And she was starting not to care about her studies - this from a girl who has wanted to be a second grade teacher since she was in kindergarten. But the main reason we had to stop her church-going activities started when she came and sat down next to me on the living room sofa and started to cry.

"What's wrong?" I asked, pulling her onto my lap.

She said, "I don't want you and Mawmaw to go to Hell."

I asked her who had told her this, and she said the minister. He said that anyone who didn't go to church regularly and doesn't believe that Jesus was the son of God would not go to Heaven. She was even worried about Grandpa and Grandma, the Baptist minister and his wife, because the church basically said, or she had understood it to say, that if you weren't in that particular denomination, you would go to Hell.

I wondered what kind of Christian this minister was behind closed doors. Probably not much of one. In Saudi Arabia, they enforce Islam with a religious police force that is supposed to "promote virtue and prevent vice." Interestingly, you could do something one day and one officer would be okay with it, and the very next day you could do exactly the same thing and be arrested. I got arrested for wearing a pair of jeans with a hole at the knee; the same pair of jeans I'd worn the week before and another officer asked me where I got them. Another time I was arrested and accused of drinking, which is strictly forbidden, and driving. Two days before the arrest, the other American teachers and I had been over to a general's home and were offered all kinds of alcohol. When I asked the general – he was drinking a large martini by this time – why he was allowed to drink and others of his faith couldn't, he said, "Because the 'common man' [I heard the quotation marks in his voice] couldn't control his alcohol consumption." It was all based on interpretation of the Koran, which the common man can't be trusted to interpret correctly.

When I was accused of drunk driving, I hadn't had anything to drink. An off duty religious police officer got mad at me for parking in what he considered to be his parking spot at the grocery store. He called in and reported that I was weaving in the car and slurring my words which I don't do even when I am drunk. I sat in jail for almost three hours, constantly asking for them to give me a breathalyzer test. They finally told me they didn't have any breathalyzers, and I had to stand in front of them and blow in their faces. I was released on my own recognizance when the complaining officer – who got the good parking place – called to say it was okay for them to let me go. In my mind, this minister was just as bad as the general or the religious police; it was all based on interpretation of the Bible, but the common man somehow forfeited the right to interpret.

Then Mamma and I were invited to attend a service and watch Allie cheer and dance. Oh my. It wasn't actually snake handling, but it was in the vicinity. There was singing and hallelujah-ing and throwing of hands up to the Lord and speaking in tongues, and one poor man in a wheel chair obviously felt something because he went up and down the aisle filled with the Holy Spirit; he would raise one hand up to the ceiling and end up going around in a circle cause he could only push with the other hand, then he'd hit a pew, and raise the other hand and start going in the opposite direction, all the while speaking gibberish – albeit holy gibberish. Then the minister came down and started "the laying of the hands" which was supposed to heal a person's illnesses and general malaise. Now Mamma and I had been kinda sorta, but not really, okay up to this point. He started coming down from the pulpit, and I looked at her and she looked at me and we started backing up; I started looking around for Allie so we could make a hasty exit. But there were so many people who wanted to be "handled" behind us and pushing forward that we didn't get far. We just kind of stood there waiting for things to subside; they didn't. The minister made his way over to us, leaving a trail of healed people behind him. He came up to me and popped me a good one on the forehead; it left a mark. I got the impression that I was supposed to cry to heaven, clasp my heart and fall to the ground; I just gave him a go-to-Hell look. He raised his hand, poised to pop Mamma a good one and she said, "Don't you hit me." And he paused in mid-pop, looked at her face, pursed his lips, then moved to the next needy individual. Mamma said that if he'd hit her, she would have decked him.

Allie didn't understand why we didn't want her to go there anymore.

<h1 style="text-align:center">17</h1>

Nine-week report cards came in. For Trisha, Megan, Allie, and Diane. Not for Caleb. According to Caleb, his teacher didn't have his because they weren't ready. I asked him if he was sure. He said yes, so I called our neighbor down the road to see if her son Mika, who was in the same grade as Caleb, got his. She said yes, he had. The entire time I was on the phone, Caleb was sitting on the couch and getting more fidgety and surlier and folding more into himself.

I hung the phone up, looked at him, and said in an exasperated voice, "Caleb, where's your report card?"

He got up and walked over to the door where he had dumped his book bag as soon as he came in, unzipped it, pulled out a piece of paper, walked back over to the end of the couch farthest from me and threw it at me. The girls left the living room abruptly, having witnessed the opening salvos in Caleb's and my war of aggression before.

I took a deep breath and unfolded it. Three F's, 2 D's, and an A in P.E. I stared at the paper, then handed it to Mamma to look at; I could feel my heart thumping in my chest and knew that my face was getting red.

"What is this?" I asked.

"Hunh?" he said, not looking at me.

"Caleb, your grades were okay on the Progress Report. What happened?"

"I dunno." His answer for everything. His shield words, impenetrable to any argument or rationale or counterstrike.

"You're gonna have to do better than this," I said pointing at the report card. While I was talking to him, Mamma got his book bag, put it on the coffee table, unzipped it all the way, and started going through it. She pulled out his folders and opened them one by one, looking at each one and putting it, still opened, on the table. In the math folder, I saw the homework we had been doing for the past three weeks, ungraded; we'd worked almost an hour a day on those pieces of paper. In the English folder, there was an essay I had helped him with last week, unmarked. I looked over at Mamma who had sat down in front of the fire place, facing us; then, I leaned my head against the back of the couch, rubbing my hand over my eyes and forehead.

"Caleb, what is this?" I asked again, hoping for something, anything. He just looked at me. "Why didn't you turn this in?" Nothing. "Caleb?" Still looking down, lips stuck out. "Caleb!!" I yelled at him.

"Stop screaming at me."

"Well, answer me," I yelled. "What is this?" pointing at the open folders, "Why didn't you turn this stuff in?"

"I dunno," he repeated.

"That's not an answer. Caleb, you failed this nine-weeks. You might fail for the year. What happened? I helped you do homework every day. Why didn't you turn it in?"

"I didn't wanna."

"That's it? That's all you have to say?" My head was in a vise, being squeezed from all sides. I stood there, fury building, clasping and unclasping my fists. "You are going to fail because you didn't want to turn your homework in?" I heard my voice explode in my ears; they could probably hear me in the next county. I pointed down the hall to the bedroom Caleb and I shared. "You get in there and unplug your video game and television and bring them in here." His school work had been the reason I got the game, positive reinforcement, because the negative reinforcement hadn't worked.

He just looked at me, lips so far out they were turning white, one side going up a little, and he mumbled something.

"What?" I said. Nothing. No movement. "What did you say, Caleb?" I asked again.

"I want my Mamma," he said and then, "You ain't gonna take my stuff. You ain't the boss of me!"

"You can't go to your Mamma."

"Why not? She wants me; she said she did."

"We don't know where she is, Caleb," Mamma said, looking at him.

"You're stuck with Mawmaw and me," I said gently, then with more force, "Now go get your game and the t.v. and bring them in here."

He looked at me with hate-filled eyes, then he looked away, a toxic silence threatening the air in the house.

"Caleb, I'm warning you. I will not tell you again. If I go get my belt, I will tear your ass up!"

He continued to stand there; I heard a ringing. It might have been a phone, or it might have been blood spurting out a broken vessel in my head. Mamma, who had been sitting at the kitchen table, got up and went down the back hall. I went to my room, got the leather belt hanging on a nail in the wall, folded it over, and walked back to the living room. I grabbed the belt just above the buckle so it slapped my wrist as I walked. It felt cold in my hand. Caleb was still standing in front of the couch.

"Go unplug your game and television and bring them in here."

His head was still down, but he looked at me from under his brow. I went over to him, pulled back the belt and hit him on the butt. Hard. His breathing got harder, but he didn't move. I hit him again, harder. Nothing. I grabbed his arm to steady myself and started hitting him again and again. He broke away and ran down the hall. I followed, getting a few extra licks in, on his butt, on his legs, on his back. He ran into the bedroom, missing the step down and falling onto the carpet. I still hit him. And hit him. Until I heard Mamma behind me say, "Garland, you're going to have a stroke."

I looked at her. I looked at the whimpering boy on the floor and asked, "Why do you make me do this? Why do you do these stupid things? What are you thinking?" I started crying, throwing the belt on the floor next to the bed and reaching down to help Caleb sit up. I sat beside him. "Caleb, baby, you can't be doing this. I told you you'd lose everything if your grades went down. Why do you do this?"

"I dunno," he said in a muffled voice because he had his arm over his face, "You don't like me; you love the girls."

"What?"

"You don't like me," he accused, sniffling and sitting up, looking at the floor. I put my hand on his shoulder.

"If I didn't like you, you wouldn't be here," I said, "I love you. I just want you to do what you're supposed to."

"I'm sorry," he said, crying again.

I took a deep breath, rubbed his head and said, "Get ready for bed."

"I'm not sleepy."

"Just do it, Caleb."

He looked at me, got up, and went to the door. He stopped, turned back to me and said, "I won't tell anybody what you did." What I did when I lost control. Me. The adult. I laid on the carpet, breathing, closing my eyes and trying to calm down.

"Garland?" I heard again, at the bedroom door this time. I looked over; Mamma was standing there. She smiled and said, "You didn't do anything wrong."

"I feel like I did. I'm supposed to be the grown up. Why does he do that to me?"

"Because he can. He knows the buttons to push; kids do that sometimes," she said.

"I can't take this; he's not going to do this to me, to us. Not to this family. If we can't control him, he won't be here."

"Garland?" this time I heard a slight quiver in her voice, "That phone call. It was Jay; Les's dead." I heard her say the words in a calm, clear voice, but they wouldn't coalesce; they clumped in the air above me.

"What?"

"His liver stopped working; what with the hepatitis and his drinking, it's amazing he lasted this long. It just stopped. They put him in the V.A. hospital, but there was nothing they could do. Jay said his skin got all orange-tinted, and he was talking out of his head about his 'sweet baby' then he died. I told John it was nothing; Les used to say that all the time in his sleep. Maybe he's in a better place now. I hope so."

It felt as if the room was closing in on me from all sides, my blood pressure soaring in the stratosphere, well on its way to the moon, "Mamma, I gotta get out of here; I'm going for a drive."

I could feel the blood pumping; there was a thump, thump, thump behind my eyes. I got in my car and started driving; south down the interstate. There was a slight chill in the air; I opened the window and let the air cool my face. Breathe. My hands gripped the steering wheel so tightly the knuckles turned white. I watched the mile markers go by. The sun was setting, a curtain descending over the world. Time to turn on the lights. Keep breathing. Thirty-five minutes. Almost there. There's the official exit, not long now. I saw the sign ahead, *"Rest Area 1 mile. No restrooms."* There. I slowed the car down and took the exit. It was dark, the almost blinding dark just after dusk before the moon or stars appear. There were two cars, I pulled past them a little way and parked. Just in front of the overflowing garbage can. I turned off my car. I looked at the trees and saw nothing except an occasional light from a car on the road behind the bit of forest. I looked in the rear view mirror. Ahead of me, I saw a white truck. I pulled on the long sleeve shirt I had in the backseat and opened the door. The light on the ceiling of the car was blinding; I kept it on just long enough for the people in the cars and the truck to see me and turned it off. I got out and shut the door, checking to make sure it was locked. I walked to the front of the car and leaned against the passenger's side, just behind the front light, hooking both of my thumbs in my pockets, emphasizing my crotch. I put one foot upon the curb, looking nonchalantly around. Garbage around the garbage can on the ground, giving off an interesting smell; the two cars just sat there, lurking. I had seen their tags as I came in; they were from around here, so it was safe. I heard the click of a door opening and turned just in time to barely make out someone getting out of the truck. The stars were starting to come out but clouds were forming, threatening even greater darkness. I watched the guy walk to the front of his truck, kick the tire on the passenger's side, the side directly in front of me, and light a cigarette. The two cars in back just sat there. Minutes took forever. He finished the cigarette, threw the butt away and stuck his hands in his pockets. He started walking towards my car. I readjusted my foot on the curb and my thumbs in my pockets.

He walked up wearing jeans with a too small jacket over an old t-shirt. Maybe 5 foot 8 and thin. Twenty? Twenty-five? Dark hair with just a hint of scruffiness on his cheeks. Good looking. He came up and nodded hello. So did I. He looked awkwardly around. I plunged my thumbs deeper in my pockets. He came closer and said, "What you up to tonight?" I didn't say anything; I took my right hand and started rubbing my crotch, answering him. He kicked the curb with the bottom of his foot and came closer. Watching me. Then he reached down, replacing my hand, rubbing the growing hardness, waiting to see if this was a set up. I watched him. I looked at the two cars. Nothing. I looked at the entrance I had just driven down and saw the lights of cars continuing on their way. I glanced over at the exit, sometimes the Highway Patrol comes up that way to try to catch deviants. Silence. And darkness. I looked back at him, my tongue licking my parched lips. He unzipped my pants, reached in and pulled out my dick. He squeezed it and said, "Nice." He bent down and licked the head. I breathed in sharply. His hand resting on my thigh, I could see his wedding band glinting in the light of the cars passing on the highway. He traced my dick with the tip of his tongue, then went back to the head, taking it all in his mouth; he worked his way down the shaft, resting at the end. His lips and nose nestling in my pubic hair. God. Heat. I saw my breath in front of me, leaving me, a spirit exiting a corpse. Abruptly, he stopped, standing back up, releasing my dick. The cold hit my wet penis hard. He smiled, unbuttoned his pants and pushed them down. He knelt in front of me, taking my dick in his mouth again and began jerking his. He stopped sucking long enough to spit in his hand. I leaned back. His lips brushed the base of my penis again; I felt the tickle of his gag reflex on the head of my dick. It felt good. There were three stars out, making a perfect triangle. Vague sounds from the woods and passing cars out on the interstate. Removing the taint. Serene. Like church at its best. He continued. Ravenous. Like me. I watched him jerk his penis; he jerked frantically then stopped. I saw two fireflies; it was too cold for them. I felt a contraction in my balls. Just what I had been waiting for. But not yet. Not until he does. That was the rule. I leaned back again, relaxing, enjoying him as he was enjoying me. Then I heard a muffled groan and saw a torrent of cum fly onto my wheel. It was okay now. I let the contraction start again. Exhale. I felt the pressure building. Building. Pushing out. Emptying me. I cum. His lips clamp tighter. He continued sucking until my dick started softening; he released me, turned his head and spit my cum on the ground next to the curb, near my feet. He got up, pulling up his pants, and buttoned them.

He looked at me again awkwardly, then leaned in and said, "You have beautiful eyes," kissing me, slightly brushing my lips with his, not too much, that would spoil the delusion; that might make him gay. He walked quickly to his truck, got in, and drove away. I zipped my pants, got in the car, and began the trip home. I felt like whistling most of the way home, but I played the radio and tried to hum along instead, filling the huge, gaping emptiness. Then the tears came, wetting my cheeks, blurring my vision, washing me. It was over. Finally.

18

One of my students had been writing in his journal, which my students have to turn in every week for a grade, about some difficulties he had been having. Now, the whole reason behind the journals was to give students an opportunity to vent – so things wouldn't build up and explode – but I was constantly amazed and surprised at what my students were willing to share.

This student had just returned from fighting in Iraq and was having trouble "lasting more than two minutes" with his girlfriend. He had never had this problem before; he had always been able to "satisfy any girl to within an inch of her life." He usually emailed his journals to me; his screen name was 9inchs4u – I couldn't help but get tickled every time I had to email him; he didn't seem embarrassed at all. In fact, he said that he just had to look at her, or touch her briefly, and he would cum. Even the second or third times. She was very frustrated; he was very frustrated. Readjustment to civilian life can be a bitch, so I told him that it might be related to his deployment in Iraq and suggested counseling. He agreed as to the cause but wouldn't go to counseling because he said every time he had been – I was guessing he had been a few times – they tried to get him on heavy medications which, according to him, "keep his dick as soft as Velveeta cheese." Well, this week he said that he had bought a special kind of cream - Pro-Long? Sta-Long? - and he was able to "go at it" for at least an hour. Of course, he thought he used too much because both he and his girlfriend lost all feeling below their navels; consequently, neither of them enjoyed it very much.

A few weeks later, 9inchs4u and his girlfriend decided to get married. She's a doctor's daughter. Because his mother worked at the college as a helper for students with disabilities and because she was a friend, we all talked a lot. Both he and his mother invited me to one of the pre-parties, claiming it would be a doozy, and since I hadn't been anywhere in forever and since the student was cute and I figured there would at least be some eye candy there for me to ogle, I said I'd go.

The day of the party, I snuck out of work about three and hurried home to change. I had been told not to wear anything fancy, but I figured that jogging pants or even jeans were out.

When I got home, the kids were already there, book bags and shoes were everywhere as were bowls and spoons and such because the first thing all of them did was head to the kitchen, each claiming to be starving. They then separate into various camps, watching television or talking on the phone or fighting; the day before Mamma said they had a Cheerios fight that took all of them thirty minutes to clean up, even after allegedly cleaning up, we found Cheerios everywhere. Well, not exactly Cheerios; they were Fruity Wheels which I bought at the Save-A-Lot market and then put in an empty Cheerios box because the kids claimed that Fruity Wheels were nasty but that they adored Cheerios. It had worked for over a year. Sometimes when the stars were properly aligned, the kids wouldn't fight and may even finish their homework early.

I went to the bedroom I shared with Caleb and sat down on my bed, trying to re-energize myself a bit when my hand landed in something wet just below my pillow. I felt around a large wet spot and then smelled my hand. Pee. The dog had peed on my bed. No, that was not quite right; a dog peed on my bed. It could have been Buster the poodle, Belle, the dachshund, Cat, the German Shepherd who is not supposed to be in the house, or T.C. (the cat); I'm not sure which actually did the deed. I think the cat was an innocent bystander because the dogs and I have issues. I yelled; Caleb came in and said that he had noticed it and had tried to clean it up. I'm not really clear on what this involved since the comforter and sheets were still on my bed leaking into my mattress. Caleb asked me where I was going; I told him and he said that he was bored and wanted his friend Billy to come over and since I was going somewhere anyway I could buy them some firecrackers. I said no to everything, and he stormed out of the bedroom yelling, "I'll get my own money for firecrackers" and slamming the door shut.

I stared at the door, watching the echo of Caleb's childish fury reverberate; then, I stood up and turned on the ceiling fan to cool things down a little. Something flew off the fan blades and landed all around the room. I looked down and saw Cheerios (Fruity Wheels) on the carpet.

Grabbing some underwear and my robe, I headed down the hall to the bathroom for a quick shower, still fuming. I never wanted animals. I never wanted to live in the country. Urban squalor was perfectly okay with me as I was never one for too much yard work.

My mother brought the poodle, Buster, with her from her house when we consolidated households; Belle lives with my sister Sara, but we now have to keep her dog everyday so "she won't feel lonely." Sara asked me one day if I would "squeeze Belle's anal gland" – which has to be done once a month – so she wouldn't have to take her to the vet; I declined. The cat, kitten really, was a gift from our next door neighbor. It seems that her cat had approximately 15 million kittens, and she was trying to pawn them off on unsuspecting individuals. We did not need any other animals, but when I came home from work, we had a kitten named T.C., for Tom Cat, on the back porch. The kids asked if they could bring him inside; again I said no. I told them that little kittens needed to be outside in the fresh air, and it would die if they brought it inside. The kitten was now inside.

Caleb knocked on the bathroom door while I was in the shower, asking to go over to Billy's house. I agreed but only if he and his sisters cleaned up the cereal off of my floor. Caleb yelled that he thought he might have seen Belle peeing on my bed. I stood in the shower, letting the hot water flow over my head and down my neck, fuming even more. I turned off the water and opened the shower curtains. Damn! I forgot to get a towel out of the cabinet. I stepped out of the shower onto the carpet, trying not to leak too much and opened the cabinet door. No towels. Only washcloths. Crap. I grabbed a couple of washcloths and hastily dried off as much as I could. Pulling on my robe, I opened the bathroom door and there sat Belle, just outside the door, watching. Because I didn't like animals in the house, these animals loved me. They followed me around, sat next to me whenever I sat anywhere, and slept -as well as urinated- on my bed. I just looked at Belle, said, "I'm mad at you!" and headed down the hall back to my bedroom. Belle followed, not even having the decency to hold her head in shame.

In the living room, I stopped to ask my mother where the towels were. She said there might be some in the other bathroom, so I headed back down the hall to check; Belle, and Buster, brought up the rear. No towels. I went back to the living room and Mamma said, "I know I washed them." Then she called Diane. Diane came in the living room and Mamma said, "You folded the towels. Where'd you put them?" Diane said, "Oh," and went into the kitchen, opened the cabinet next to the refrigerator and there were all of the towels, stacked neatly.

"Why did you put them in the kitchen?" I asked, exasperated.

"I didn't want to have to carry them back to the back," she said, using her child-logic, "I wanted to go outside and play." Which made no sense although this was the reason we moved to the country.

For years, all I heard was how wonderful living in the country would be and how great it would be for the kids. I remembered years ago my grandmother inviting me to come with her to pick peas. There we were in the true Mississippi summer heat, bent over those insidious pea plants, plucking away. Every few minutes, my grandmother would look at me, grin, and say, "Isn't this fun?" I think she might have even sung, but I'm not sure as I was gulping for air and attempting to wipe sweat off of my face.

Maybe I should have suggested picking peas for the kids. In my opinion, the only time the country is okay is when I'm looking at it through triple insulated windows, in full out air conditioning which is not only cooling the air but also filtering out 99.9% of the pollen and pet dander. Nature. I couldn't think of anything I enjoyed less. Ever.

My mother, who handed me one of the towels and took all of the others out of the cabinet, was completely enamored with this place. She said that all she'd ever wanted in life was a house in the country with a fireplace and a lot of kids. She never thought she'd get that because of her choices in men, but she's been given a second chance.

Anything else she could deal with. I watched her walk down the hall, dividing the towels between bathrooms, and humming to herself, followed admiringly by Buster, Belle and even T.C.

I got back to my room, took the comforter and sheets off of my bed and threw them in the utility room; luckily, nothing had gotten on the mattress itself, or I would have had to burn it. I got dressed quickly in a nice white shirt and tan, ever ready, no-iron Dockers and ran out to my car.

Even though I had a map and general directions, I didn't have a Sherpa guide, so it took me longer to get to the party than I'd thought. I didn't think I had ever been to this part of town. At least not to the residential section. I drove by wonderful house after wonderful house. This student obviously chose his bride well. I turned down this one street and saw a lot of cars parked. Going further down, there was one of the biggest houses I'd ever seen; there were two very muscular young men in golf carts, directing people to available parking places. I parked where they directed, trying nonchalantly to keep the two guys in my rear view mirror, got out, and proceeded into the house. People actually lived in this place! The door opened into a relatively small foyer, with a small dark table in the center which had a large vase of daisies on it. Going around the table, I went through another door. Oh my. It opened into a very large room with two staircases circling up to the second floor; centered at the base of the staircases was another doorway. Just over the doorway was a large painting with some sort of crest on it, and I could make out the letters B and S done very ornately in green and gold. Through the central doorway, I could see another large room. There was an ice sculpture of a swan in the center of a table arranged with all sorts of goodies.

Not seeing my host or his mother, I grabbed a plate, filled it to almost overflowing as I had not eaten today and was starving and then got a wonderful blue drink that had an umbrella in it. "I'm in heaven," I thought as I saw yet another good looking guy. I continued to stand and eat, basking in the glow one gets when one is almost completely satisfied when I heard someone behind me say, "Hey, Garland, I didn't know you knew Brett and Simpsy? Can you believe they've been married twenty years? They are the sweetest couple."

I turned to see one of the ladies I worked with. Who were Brett and Simpsy? Any reply I might have made dribbled out my ear and puddled on one of the tasteful Persian rugs or so I imagined. I just smiled, thankful that she was absorbed in the goodies and the drinks too. She turned her back to me to talk to someone else, and I hurried to another table. This was not the pre-party. Then I took in more of my surroundings; all of the other men were in very nice suits and ties and the ladies were wearing evening apparel and pearls or some such. Which way did I come in? I finished my plate and my drink (waste not) and hurried to my car.

I looked at the directions and the address again and tried to see the two muscular guys in the golf cart (again, waste not). My party was two blocks over. I drove on over and parked all by myself. There were no guys, good looking or otherwise, in golf carts. I went in; my student and his mother and even his fiancé couldn't have been nicer, but it really wasn't the same. I kind of wished I had known either Brett or Simpsy. Oh well. It did get me dressed up and out of the house.

I left shortly afterward because I had a headache. As I was driving home, Megan called and said that one of her friends who lives in Billy's neighborhood called and told her that Caleb and Billy were going door to door asking for donations for Caleb's sick grandmother who was "in the hospital and needs a lot of stuff done."

Looks like he was trying to buy his own firecrackers.

God, I'm lonely.

19

"Garland?" I heard the heavily accented Moroccan voice on the other end of the phone line say; the syllables came out with, at least in my mind, erotic precision. Then he said, "How are you?" Only one person talked like that. I had every nuance of that voice memorized. Goose bumps came up on my arms, and my heart started racing, vying for attention with my breathing.

"Bellalami," I breathed, more of a sigh than a statement. A name out of my ancient history. He had been the manager of a resort-hotel in Taif, Saudi Arabia. He'd also been my boyfriend for four years. Not that he'd ever admit that. It just wasn't talked about in a religious community.

Morocco was more open than Saudi Arabia, but being gay was still a death sentence in both countries. And there was the shunning of the families of the offending parties.

We had watched movies together, played tennis together, and ate dinner at least five times a week together. And we had slept together; I couldn't keep my hands off of him, at least in private. And I loved kissing him. But we weren't boyfriends. He was engaged. Had been since he was in school. Some arranged thing. We didn't talk about it much. He went to her two weeks a year when he had his vacation and talked to her every Friday morning (our Sunday). The rest of the time, he was mine. And I was his. He had left Saudi a month before I did and was now the manager of a very large hotel in Dubai in the United

Arab Emirates. A short drive from the university I had wanted to work at in Oman.

"Bellalami Asir," I said again, my voice catching in my throat as it did whenever I said his name, "You sound good. How are you?"

"More than fine," he said, "I called your house and your mother said you were working. I do not think she understood anything I said." He hated when people claimed they didn't understand him; he thought his pronunciation was perfect. He continued, "She gave me this number. I hope it is okay to call."

"Sure it is. How is Dubai?"

"Good. Growing. Not like Saudi. More open."

I laughed. "I've heard that. Dubai's the place to be."

"Like Oman."

"True," I said, painfully. There's always danger in reopening old wounds or old wants or old hopes. I'd already been in Saudi a few years when we met. I used to go to the hotel he managed on Thursday mornings (our Saturdays) for a cappuccino or six. The hotel was situated overlooking three awe-inspiring mountain peaks. What a view. Then I saw him. God, that man was beautiful. I don't even remember what I said to him when we met. I get very tongue tied around good looking guys, especially the ones I'm interested in. I don't think I said anything; I just made some consonant noises. Whatever it was, he laughed. We "courted" for six months, slowly circling each other, drawing the other out little by little, being absolutely sure of each other in a place that would put a person in jail over even the accusation of deviance. Then we were sure. He helped make Saudi okay.

The silence lengthened. I didn't know what to say to this man who had become a stranger.

"I wanted to see how you are doing," he said finally, filling the chasm between us.

"I'm fine. Work. Kids. One day after another." We used to talk to each other about anything. Great arguments about politics or religion or Madonna's latest cd. Then we got to make up. I loved the making up part. I miss the making up part.

"Yes, that is how it always is," he agreed, not having a clue what I was going through here. He didn't quite sound like himself.

"Are you okay?"

"Sure. Why not? This is a good time for me. Work is good," Then his voice changed a little, "And I am getting married."

My stomach dropped. "Oh," I said, "To Fatima?" He used to have her picture on the night stand by his bed, very beautiful; he always put it in the drawer when I stayed over.

"Who else?" he asked, sounding a little amused.

"When?"

"Tomorrow, a very traditional marriage."

"Oh," I said again, "What time is it there?" Curious. It was early afternoon here, almost time to go home.

"Almost 11p.m. I am about to go to bed." His words hung in the air like a heady perfume, then he continued hesitantly, "It is a big day tomorrow."

"I hope everything goes well. And that you're happy."

"Very happy," he agreed, but did I imagine that his voice didn't echo his statement? "As is Fatima and our parents. I only get three weeks off of work. But it is time for this new chapter in my life."

Silence. A wall of silence. A universe of silence. A chapter of silence. The biggest fight we ever got into was over his engagement. It had started out kind of joking. We had been in bed at the time, after a love making session that had made my heart skip and had left us both sweaty and gasping for breath; I told him that he would never be happy with a woman. That it would be a damned shame. And that he wasn't being fair to Fatima. He'd never been with a woman before and, judging by what he liked to do or have done to him in bed, that part of their lives would never be fulfilling for him or her.

I shouldn't have said that because he came from that peculiar Mediterranean viewpoint that the passive man was the queer. He would be very passionate in bed but then feel horribly guilty because what he liked branded him with a big scarlet Q. I've never seen him that angry. He said that he loved her and would never disgrace his family by "being a faggot." That was the last time the subject was discussed.

I felt the cold plastic of the phone in my hand and said the only thing I could think of, "I'm happy for you."

"Are you really?"

"Sure Lami, I want you to be happy." The silence returned. We'd tried writing letters and calling for a while when I first got here but then the inevitable drifting apart had taken place, glaciers once united, but now caught in different currents. In my mind's eye, I could barely make out his face in the distance.

"Well, I just wanted to see how you are doing. I should go now," he said, this time I heard a tremor in his voice, "I missed your voice, your laugh. You could call me sometime, you know."

"I will," I said, knowing that I wouldn't. I was a character from his last chapter, not the new one. "Eat an extra piece of wedding cake for me, okay?"

"I will eat a piece and think only of you," he said, then with even more emphasis, "Only you." There was a pause, then, "Goodbye, my Garland."

"Goodbye, my Lami." I said, not trusting my voice, but I did manage to get out, "You be happy, you hear?"

People who have lost arms or legs say that they can sometimes feel pain in the limb that is no longer there. Phantom pain. It's true for the heart as well.

20

I drove and drove trying to find the place. I took the turn Google had kindly suggested and found myself in a very bad part of town. Lots of abandoned warehouses and such. Streetlights that looked iffy at best. "5th Street, 6th Street, 7th Street" and I turned right. There it was. JJ's. There was a huge sign out front with a long high-heeled leg advertising "JJ's Girl-o-rama." With a note underneath which said, "The best ladies in the South." Just where I wanted to be. 9inchs4u originally wanted me to come to his wedding. I told him I couldn't because I had to do something for the kids (an all-purpose excuse); really I didn't have any money to get a gift. When I told him I couldn't come to the wedding, he said, "Then you'll come to the bachelor's party. All my guy friends are still in the army and can't be here; it'll be fun." Then he leaned in and whispered, "We're having it at JJ's." I couldn't come up with an excuse fast enough. At first, 9inchs had wanted me to meet at his place where his brother Brandon, a cousin who was also named Brandon and was very cute, and his best friend Lee were getting together for "a few shots to begin the festivities." I did get out of that.

I parked my car with the other two or three cars in the parking lot and waited. And waited. Many very interesting and scary individuals walked by. One in particular kept walking by my car, smiling and cupping her breast. She was wearing a long coat but not much else. I breathed a sigh of relief when I saw their car pulling into the parking lot. They were very rowdy. 9inchs staggered over and gave me a bear hug; he was thrilled that I came.

He said, "I'm gonna be a married man tomorrow. This is my last night of freedom. Whoooooeeeeeeson!!" The last was picked up by the others until I felt that I should shout as well.

"Wooooeeeeee!" I semi-shouted with a fist in the air for emphasis; I'm a manly man. I had not put in my contact lenses, so I kept nervously pushing my glasses up on my nose and followed 9inchs, the Brandons and Lee through the front door into the darkest establishment I think I had ever been in. I pushed my glasses up again and looked around as my eyes adjusted to the lack of light. Okay. It was a lot smaller than I thought. But about as dirty. And there was an odor, Pine Sol with something underneath that tickled at and then threatened my nose. Directly in front of us was a bar with about ten stools, only the outer ones occupied. Behind the bar was a stage-like area with three poles evenly spaced coming down from the ceiling and a curtain behind them. Along the walls were four additional poles ending in tables for patrons to sit at and get "those private dances." A dart board half-heartedly hung on the wall just past the last pole, a precarious location if you ask me. A pool table sat menacingly in the very back next to the door that led to a backroom for even more privacy; all of which was probably very expensive.

9inchs sat at the bar in the center, on his right sat Brandon and then Lee. On his left sat Cute Brandon and me. An exceedingly large woman came up and gave us each three Jell-O shots of something. She left and the lights came up on stage. Then JJ's ladies emerged. Three of them. Large women. Who had definitely seen better days. Even the subdued lighting didn't help. One was very black, one was kinda black, and one wasn't. They each wore very high heels and had hair and nails that were impeccable. I drank a shot. Cute Brandon's eyes got big and just kind of stayed that way; he didn't even blink much. The music started and the gyrations began. I moved closer to Brandon and drank another shot. All of the ladies were wearing star shaped pasties of varying sizes and wore g-strings. At least I think so, the one who wasn't had rolls of fat that obscured the g-string, and I refused to let my eyes wander; she just kept flouncing hither and yon in front of other Brandon and Lee. At one point, she put her back to the pole, suggestively swished her hips and gave them both a come-hither look.

Kinda Black was dancing in front of me and Cute Brandon; she attempted to squat down while keeping time to the music; when she finally made that last little plunge all of the way down onto the balls of her feet, I heard her knees crack; then, she visibly and with a good bit of effort pulled herself back up on the pole.

The very black lady with life-threatening breasts and itty bitty pasties over what had to be very large areoles was dancing up a storm in front of 9inchs. He was eating it up. He had downed all of his shots and was whooping and hollering. She went down on her knees and bent forward, and he buried his face in her breasts, making bad-breathing, slurping sounds. She looked as if she were in all kinds of ecstasy and let him bury deeper.

Not to be outdone, Kinda Black went down on her knees, legs spread wide open, grabbed my glasses and rubbed them inside of her g-string. With a pouty face she put my Calvin Klein glasses back on my face. I think that was when I grabbed Cute Brandon's knee for no apparent reason that I could think of. Then she put that same finger that had just come out of her g-string under cute Brandon's nose for him to sniff, which he did and then coughed. She took the finger and put it between her teeth, pouting again as if she were a model on the cover of a high fashion magazine, then leaned forward and said in a surprisingly deep voice, "I do lap dances."

I closed my eyes tightly out of fear of infection but not before seeing that the lenses were very smeared with god-knows-what. I needed a wipe, but all I had was a piece of paper towel in my pocket; I took them gingerly off of my face, trying not to contaminate anything else. And trying not to get sick. Oh my. Cute Brandon's eyes had gotten so big that I thought he might have sprained something and that they'd never go back to normal. Then, I looked down and realized my hand had somehow moved to his upper thigh. Oops.

I ran to the bathroom and tried to clean my glasses, but there was no hot water and no soap in the dispenser. I rinsed them off with cold water, slung the excess off and wrapped them in toilet paper and stuffed them in my pocket.

I got back out, not being able to see anything and made my way back to the bar, squinting at cute Brandon; he'd finished all of his shots and moved his chair as far from mine as was polite. Great. The ladies had left, but 9inchs confided to us that they would give everyone a "private showing" if we really wanted. Then the curtain opened revealing another pole with a chair directly behind it, the chair's back touching the pole. The main event had started. I saw a rather large blur come out on stage and sit in the chair, her back to us. The music started and she stood and started gyrating. Belly dancing, acid rock style. She turned, grabbed the chair and pulled it up in front of 9inchs. Still gyrating. He was in his own zone, oblivious to anything else. She was just a dancing when one of her pasties fell and landed right in front of me. She turned to look for it, saw me instead and yelled, "Hey Mr. Stewart! You my favorite teacher!"

21

There were moments when I knew that if I got the least bit of sympathy from anyone I would crack like an egg. I didn't mind things being difficult; I just never understood how difficult they could be or why they had to be difficult all the time. I felt my soul eroding away under the constant drip, drip, drip of life. I wanted to leave. I wanted to run back overseas. A person in the midst of a self pity frenzy might consider it rude, possibly even counter-productive, for a person to try to cheer them up. There I was absolutely positive that of the 6 billion people on the face of the planet that God had picked me to torture. I had no life, I had no money, the kids hated me; I would be turning forty and had no boyfriend nor any hope of one because to get a boyfriend one had to actually be in a place where one might meet possibilities.

That was my frame of mind when I saw, or rather heard, Sissy.

My relationship with Sissy went back to my second year at the college when she suddenly appeared at my office door. She was a not small woman -big boned as polite people say- about 58, with bleached blonde hair and a gravelly voice that brought to mind too many nights spent in smoke filled bars. She was also very, very intelligent. She came to my office the second week of the semester saying she had to get into my already overflowing English class. As she said, this was her first class in college and somehow, even though she'd been told she wasn't the only non-traditional student enrolled and that every class was a mixture of ages and sexes, this English class she was in had been filled mainly with eighteen year old females wearing spaghetti straps and high heels; Sissy swore that if she didn't get in my Saturday morning class she was "liable to kill someone." To this day, I don't know what made me let her in my class. Yes, I do; I'm a sucker for needy people. But she was one of those students who makes teaching a joy and an honor. Not at first, mind you. She bitched about everything: "I hate getting up this early. Why the Hell can't they make class times suitable for decent drinking folks?" or "I don't see why we have to type our papers on the computer; I'm almost 60, and I hate those damned things!"

One day I had had enough, so I said, "Sissy, shut up, plant your ass in that chair and just write that damn paper." No one dared make a sound. Sissy's eyes got big; then, a grin spread across her face and she sat down and wrote the damn paper. I never had another problem. She yelled at me, and I yelled right back, which is not what they taught in those education classes I had had to take. I called her the Biker Chick from Hell. And she did little things to try to needle me. Like when I told the class that they could probably add five or ten points to their essay grades if they made me laugh, and she wrote an paper on the most unusual places she'd ever had sex. I laughed my ass off; her top three places were her church, the hood of her boyfriend's car, and the cemetery.

None of her other teachers understood her, and she made them pay; one of her history teachers told her class that he wanted them to be able to discuss history on the subway and she said, "Man, there ain't no subway in Toomsuba, Mississippi." She got an F on the first test in that class , but she got her revenge. Her history teacher was from up north, and Sissy liked to tell him little tidbits of made up Southern history. He brought up the Ku Klux Klan one evening, and she looked up from taking notes and said, "What you got against the Klan?" She said he was shocked almost speechless. She then told him that the Klan had been "integrated since desegregation and that they took turns burning things in different races' yards." She went on to tell him that they were going to burn a cross in a nice Guatemalan couple's yard that very night. He actually believed her, at least for a while.

She had other methods of revenge as well. She would walk past any teacher she hated and fart. She said they were "silent but deadly" and that she could do it on command. I told her I better not smell anything funny around her. So far I've had her in three classes, and I've gotten to watch her blossom, relatively speaking. No, she was not typical at all. She left school in the tenth grade to marry a man who drank heavily and beat her. And she lived in that for thirty-seven years. One day, as she says, she "woke up" and realized that she'd married a cast-iron bastard. They tried counseling because they had three children together and "that's what you do after being with someone that long" but then he got a restraining order against her.

"A restraining order? What did you do?" I asked one day after class when she told me the story.

"He *claimed* I was drugging him," she said.

"Were you?" Not putting anything past a woman who would threaten to kill young scantily dressed women.

"Hell yeah," she said. "That counselor we was going to said I needed an antidepressant or I was gonna have a hissy fit. I decided he needed the Zoloft more'n me so I started putting it in his coffee every morning." She grinned fiercely. "Best six months of our marriage. Then he saw me one morning and got suspicious. He stopped drinking coffee. Claimed the caffeine made him jittery." She stopped for a moment, then continued, "That piece of shit."

She left everything and moved into a shelter. God, what a brave woman. She worked the 3 p.m. to 11 p.m. shift at Chevron for minimum wage.

My gas light came on while I was on the interstate going home, so I decided to stop because I knew the car wouldn't make it out to my house and back on the fumes in the tank. I pulled off of the interstate at my exit, and slowed because the light had just turned to yellow. As I came to a complete stop, I noticed a man by the highway with a large sign that said, "REPENT THE END IS NEAR" which complemented my mood exactly. I pulled into the Chevron station, stopped the car at the pumps, got out and started pumping gas when Sissy yelled at me through the intercom on the gas pumps, "Hey Mr. Stewart! I'm gonna be taking your class next semester. Are you ready?"

I had to smile. If she could bear her burden, mine was no problem. I said with a fake put-upon sigh, "I guess I am, but if you fart anywhere near me it will affect your grade." If we were coming to the end of days, I knew exactly who I wanted with me. And I went home and dove back into my family.

22

Caleb missed football practice one Saturday morning because he didn't tell me they were having football practice; then, he got mad at me for not taking him. This meant I was at home when Lynn walked to the house.

The guy she was living with had kicked her out. They were fighting because he got paid and instead of buying groceries, he bought drugs. Lynn said she'd been eating grits for a week and didn't have any toilet paper. And he spent his whole paycheck on crack. Anyway, he kicked her out of that trailer and wouldn't let her get her shoes. She walked six miles on the hot pavement to get to our house, sat for exactly 23 minutes complaining about the huge blisters on her feet, and then wanted Mamma to drive her back. She smelled like a brewery. And cigarette smoke. She never stayed at our house long because she claimed we had too many rules. There were only three: 1) No drugs, 2) No drinking, and 3) No smoking because Allie has asthma. But these were too much for her; she couldn't last very long without a drink or a cigarette or a hit of something.

She used to talk to the kids a lot, but I kind of limited that since she got Trisha's boyfriend on the phone and asked him how big his dick was and told him that he should make sure to be gentle when he was screwing her. I knew at least two of the kids secretly called her, but I couldn't stop that. That was a battle no one would win. The kids were in the process of getting to un-know her. They didn't mention her much although I know they worried. Add to that the stealing.

Whenever we knew Lynn was coming over, we had to hide everything; the last time she was at our house, she took Mamma's engagement ring. We had to lock the freezer and put all of Mamma's prescriptions in the closet in my room. Lynn had a bad habit of going through the house, picking up various things and then going to pawn them or sell the prescriptions to somebody.

She also embarrassed them. Diane was on a school trip a few weeks back, and the bus went past a garbage dump where Lynn and her boyfriend of the moment were dumpster diving. One of the chaperones said, "Look at those filthy people! The police should come and run everyone of them out of here."

I watched her there at the kitchen table where she'd immediately sat when she came in, ignoring Diane's outstretched arms, and Allie's and Caleb's looks begging for some kind of acknowledgement. Her face was gaunt, and she had rotten teeth; this couldn't be my sister. She called Mamma every day or so; I saw who was calling on the caller I.D. and didn't answer, but Mamma always did. She got exasperated with Lynn, and she was usually crying when she hung up. I got so mad. It was a running argument between us. Mamma talked to Lynn, gave her rides to different places, and even took food to her. I said we were just enabling her, and we should stop any contact with her. But Mamma wouldn't. The same thing in her that caused her to take in the kids wouldn't let her do that to her daughter.

It burned me up. "Why do you let her do that to you? Why don't you just hang up? Or not even take the call," I asked and asked, thinking that at some point a person has to just close the door.

Mamma didn't answer right away; she was still wiping her eyes and blowing her nose. Then she looked over at me and said as if she were talking to a very small child, "Because whenever I talk to her, I never know if this will be the last time I get to talk to her. Every time the phone rings I expect it to be someone telling me they've found her body by the side of the road somewhere. It would kill me to know that I didn't talk to her that one last time." Who says addicts only destroy themselves? I can point to a path of destruction leading straight to my door.

23

After her experience at the church, Allie decided to be our family's second cheerleader. Then, she started having a problem; she appeared to be unable to do the "pelvic roll," a move that, according to Megan, would be essential to her cheerleading career. So Allie had been practicing said move, all week, everywhere. To the point where her teacher sent a note home wanting me to talk to her as to the "appropriateness" of attempting this classic move in such places as the line for lunch or at the blackboard after she's correctly answered a math problem. The teacher thinks this is most distracting especially for the soon-to-hit puberty boys in her class. I broached the subject with Allie, saying in effect, "honey, wait til you get home and you can pelvic roll 'til the cows come home," and she appeared to understand, but one is never really sure about children. Forget the crisis in the Middle East or America's huge budget deficit or even trying to come up with the one hundred and thirty dollars for her cheerleading outfit, including the pompoms. Mostly, it's not the big things that hold a family together; it's the moment-to-moment, day-to-day conversations and actions that build, or destroy, trust and hope and understanding. The world would be a better place if everyone could perfect a pelvic roll. Maybe even her teacher. Definitely her teacher.

"Can Mika come up to play?" Caleb asked. It was Wednesday afternoon and, although Mika lives down the road, there's a hard and fast rule that no one comes up during the week.

"No," I said.

"Why not?" he whined, volume increasing steadily, "I don't have anyone to play with, and I have to go to practice soon."

"I know you have practice. At five," I said, trying for logic even though I knew it was a lost cause, "That's why he can't come up now. You have to finish your homework and get your stuff out for tomorrow." This because he was so exhausted after practice, it was all we could do to get him bathed and in bed.

"I already told him he could," he said, eyes full of hatred.

Oh great. Now I got to be the bad guy. A part I seemed destined to play. I could tell Mika (who would be here in a few minutes) that he couldn't stay or Caleb got his way (doing something he knew not to do). This had been the kind of encounter Caleb and I have been having lately. He did something to provoke me, and it quickly degenerated into a shouting match; I know I was supposed to be the adult, but I wasn't. I made Caleb call Mika and tell him that he couldn't come up this afternoon but maybe he might be able to come up sometime over the weekend. Caleb glared at me the whole time and blurted out every word like he was being forced at gunpoint. He mouthed the words, "I hate you" under his breath; I pretended not to see. God, how he hated me. I had just appeared in the house from nowhere and started taking care of him; at least that was how he probably saw it.

When he was six, I'd run through the house chasing him and Allie and Diane. I'd tickle them when I caught one. They would squeal with laughter. Caleb especially. One night at dinner which we had on the coffee table because we didn't have a dining room table, he and I started playing like this. Mamma said, "Would ya'll stop that and eat. Caleb, you wanted that corn, now you eat it." I sat next to him on the couch and would reach over and tickle him every once in a while. He loved it. When I realized that he was just playing with his food, we went at it full force. I pretended to stick my finger in my nose and told him that I was going to make him eat a booger. He would wriggle away, laughing hysterically.

Then, I "played guitar" on him. I would get him to stiffen his body and then I'd lay him across my lap and strum his chest and belly while I attempted to sing badly which is not a problem for me. I continued joking and tickling him and then I told him again that I was going to make him eat a booger. He thought that was the funniest thing in the world. And I tickled and he fought a little. When I really started tickling him a lot, he lay on the couch and closed his eyes as he was trying to squirm away; as soon as he closed his eyes, I pretended to reach in my nose to get a booger, then I reached down and got a piece of corn off of his plate and put it in his mouth. He came up off of the couch, gagging and spitting. I was laughing so hard that I couldn't speak. The girls were laughing too. I think that was when things started to go sour.

He would be a teenager soon and start his growth spurt. I didn't think I would survive his adolescence. But there were glimmers of hope. The other day, Caleb, Allie, Diane and I were in Walmart, my second home, eating at McDonalds which is the kids' favorite restaurant. We were sitting there waiting for our orders and having an okay enough time when an old man passed by. He had a cup of coffee in his hand, and when he went to sit down, the table wobbled and he spilled coffee all over the table. Caleb got up, got some napkins and went over and helped him clean it up. Then he came back, sat down, and continued eating. No muss. No fuss. No shouting. Little glimmers that filled my heart to overflowing.

24

I was asked to teach another class at the prison, and this time I knew it would be very different. The biggest difference was that I had a better idea of what to expect. I know that you couldn't really know what to expect from people who technically weren't sane, but at least I would be more comfortable in the prison surroundings. I could have said no, but I really needed the money and, truth be told, crazy people fascinate me. They really do. And I can't leave it alone; I have to ask questions. Really, most people on that side of the great sanity divide are very intelligent, and as long as you go along with their version of reality, they don't get violent. I just asked questions, smiled, and filed away their answers.

In addition to my better attitude, I had a new classroom. The upside of that was that it was a very nice classroom in which the door didn't automatically lock when anyone breathed on it; the downside was that it was right across the hallway from the nurses' station where they dispensed medication. Most of the prisoners really needed their meds although there were exceptions.

Last time I taught out there, one of the student seemed perfectly lucid so I said, "I hope you don't mind me saying anything, but you seem relatively okay. Are you psychotic or anything?"

He laughed and said in a low conspiracy heavy voice, "Nah, I'm okay. I just got tired of the penitentiary, so I tol' everybody that I was seeing a dog 'til they put me away. I like it here better."

"They give some pretty potent medication. Aren't you afraid

it might do something to your...?" I asked, tapping the side of my head.

"They's ways round that. Ya don' have to take nothing ya don' want to."

Or do anything you didn't want to do, it seems.

Fourteen students showed up for class. There were fifteen on roll but one was in twenty-three-hour lockdown; that's twenty-three hours locked in a cell, with one hour out for exercise. For the lay person, that's twenty-three hours for not-stupid guys to think of mischief; I went in there once last time I taught here to give a final exam. There were streams of water – and other things – floating across the floor because a few of the prisoners had stopped up their toilets; they hurled various liquids at anyone who came through. My student this semester was in lockdown for throwing something heavy at a guard. I probably wouldn't be seeing him anytime soon.

I started class and gave my opening smoke-and-mirror routine; every teacher is different; one teacher on campus used to say, "I am like God. I have all of the answers. You want all of the answers. You simply have to figure out a way to get them." That teacher didn't last very long. I went through everything, assignments and homework, giving the prisoners double or triple the homework I give regular students because these students need lots of work to fill the time. They were very bored and do every scrap of homework I assign which simply didn't happen on the main campus.

I got them started on their introductory paragraphs then I walked around the room, helping and offering advice as needed. One of the students, who called himself Special Kay, threw his pencil down on his paper and gave a loud, long, disgusted sigh.

"It ain't no use! I can't think!" he cried.

I walked over to him and said in my most helpful teacher's voice, "It's just a first paragraph. Take your time. I'm not looking for perfection. You're here to learn."

"No, I can't think I tell ya. Damn! I wish that cat'd bring my head back."

"Beg pardon?" I asked ingeniously.

He looked at me like I was the stupidest person in the known universe, took his hand and started feeling around his head, then he said, "Can't ya see I ain't got a head?"

"Hmmm," I thought for a second and then I asked what I thought was an obvious question. "What's that you're touching?" since there seemed to be something there on his shoulders and I was more than certain it was his head.

"It's a dome [he actually spread the word out and made about five syllables out of it] – made of plastic. I had to have something to cover the hole the cat left. I can't wait for him to bring it back."

"Well, where is the cat?" I asked, looking around for emphasis.

"Round here somewhere. I tried to catch it, but it's jus' too fast!"

"Whose cat is it?" I asked.

"My girlfriend's. Really my ex-girlfriend's cause she was sleeping around." Then he looked at me, winked and added, "She was always saying that I was the cutest thing she'd ever seen, and she wanted something to remember me by."

I told him that if he really wanted to he could work on his paragraph in his jail cell so he left.

After he walked out the door, another prisoner said, "That fucker's crazy!"

25

On Monday, the house was like a disturbed ant hill on acid. The kids were supposed to get all of their clothes out, including socks, the night before; even when I watched them do this, it didn't stop the general hyperactive pandemonium that struck our house almost every morning but especially Mondays.

"She's wearing my shirt!"

"I hate eggs!"

"Where are my shoes?"

"Make Caleb stop pinching me!"

"That's not my book bag!"

There was this maelstrom going on that I tried to be the calm center of. On this particular morning, during that daily cataclysmic event that I called "getting ready for school and driving me to drink," I was trying to escape out the back door because I was late for work when my mother thrust two bags of garbage at me and said for me to look around on my way to my car because she thought something was eating Cat's food. The dog did look like she was getting skinnier, but I didn't see anything out of the ordinary on my way to my car. And I really didn't know what to look for anyway.

At work, the other Multicultural Advisor told me that she thought we should start a step team. I told her that I would be more than happy to lend my expertise; she said, "That's okay. We'll swap out being in the dance studio; they must have an advisor there at all times."

On Tuesday, I went out to the prison and continued my ongoing argument with Special Kay. He refused to do his homework because he wanted me to call the dog pound about his head. He thought he saw the cat that stole his head everywhere. In fact, he could be rude about the whole thing; I would be standing, talking to him and suddenly he just ran off, sometimes while he was in the middle of a sentence, because he thought he saw that cat . And he would make these, according to him, humorous remarks. I might ask him, "Where's your homework?" and he would get this big grin on his face and say, "The pussy got it!" and then laugh hysterically.

Believe it or not, this reminded me of the kind of humor that I ran into in Saudi Arabia. I'm not saying that there was no humor; I am saying that it is very difficult for someone outside of a particular culture to understand what made something funny to a group of people. A typical joke in Saudi might go something like this:

"A man has four bananas. He gives one to his father, one to his brother, and one to the imam [holy man]." Then he'd look at me expectantly.

"Where's the last banana?" I'd ask on cue.

"In your ass!" he'd say, accompanied by an almost maniacal "ha ha ha ha!." I still don't get it.

It was very distracting when Special Kay acted like this; crazy people can be completely unreasonable at times. And to add insult to injury there had arisen an additional problem in that class. One of the prisoners had taken to sitting in the back of the room and quite obviously playing with himself. The other students didn't seem to mind, but I didn't really know how to approach this problem, as I was sure it had never happened to me before and believe me I would have noticed. Should I have gone up to his desk, leaned over and whispered, "Pardon me but could you please not fondle yourself during class? Wait 'til you get back to your cell"? Was there an etiquette book that covered this?

Aside from that, the guy was really a good writer.

Then I made it home and all of the kids, even a couple that I was pretty sure that I had never seen before, ran to my car, yelling and screaming because they said they had just seen this huge bird that ran away when they started chasing it. I dutifully looked where they pointed and mumbled something inane; my mind still on the step team, Special Kay and Hand Job. I was absolutely exhausted, so I helped with homework and went to bed, thankful that there was no cheerleading or football practice.

On Thursday, I got up, shaved, took a shower, and was sitting at the kitchen table drinking a cup of coffee and enjoying practically the only quiet time of my day when I looked out the back window, and I swear that I saw an emu eating the dog's food.

"That's it," I thought to myself, taking another sip of dark roast, "I've finally gone crazy." Pretty soon, I was pretty sure, I'd stop shaving and performing other basic hygiene and would start mumbling and wandering around in my robe, peeing on the azaleas. It sounded tranquil. Then I saw the emu nip playfully at Cat who didn't seem to mind at all and, in fact, seemed to be very friendly with the creature.

The sheriff's department told me when I called them to report the emu that this was now a common occurrence in our area. A few years back, many people had emu farms, thinking that raising emus would make them rich; when that didn't happen, they just freed the emus and let them go wild. Great.

I got to the prison and had only thirteen out of sixteen students show up for class. Special Kay wasn't there. The other students told me that Kay was in lock down. He'd been there since Tuesday night and there were explicit instructions that he could not be around any uniformed staff as this would "set him off." Even though he was one of my favorite students, I did breathe a sigh of relief. Then Ms. Wilson, head of instruction at the prison, came in with Special Kay right behind her. He was just a fussing. About everything. They weren't treating him right. His rights had been violated. He was being discriminated against. Ms. Wilson was just nodding her head and saying, "Uh huh" every couple of seconds. She walked him to a seat and, as she was leaving, looked at me and mouthed the words "Be careful," and left. Special Kay just sat there staring at me. And staring. And staring. Which was actually okay because I remembered reading somewhere something that said that people who looked you in the eyes were less likely to kill you. Then I looked at the back of the room and saw Hand Job untucking his shirt so he could begin his two o'clock performance.

I began teaching the lesson on commas and was standing at the front of the classroom at the white board when the door opened. A thin, little man dressed in prison garb came in. He had to be at least fifty and had just a few teeth in his mouth and just a few hairs on his head that he combed over from the side. He also had a broom; it looked like he'd been sweeping the hall outside of the classroom.

He wasn't one of my students, so I stopped what I was doing and said, "Can I help you?"

He came to the front of the classroom, leaned his broom against the wall, turned back to me and the class and said, "I'd like to dedicate this song to my mamma even though the bitch never did a damn thing for me." Then he started singing "One day at a Time, Sweet Jesus," going through two verses of the worst prescription-drug-enhanced rendition of that song that I had ever heard. But I smiled in a professional, if not confused, manner. When he finished, he picked up his broom, gave a slight bow and said, "Thank you."

"No, thank you," I said. He left the classroom, and I turned to my students and asked, "Who was that?"

"Oh, that's Crazy Eddie," Special Kay said, "he eats garbage."

On Friday, I went to my regular on campus classes. I was teaching a Study Skills class where I said things such as, "Read your textbooks" or "Take Notes" or "Don't sleep in class" – the basics; I'd talked about thirty-five minutes when I asked, "Does anyone have any questions?"

A young lady in the back of the room raised her hand and said, "Why have you been wearing those tight shirts?" I love modern education.

Ms. Wilson called and asked if I could stop back by the prison and go through the orientation I had been promised when I first went out there a few years ago; she said something about some paperwork they had to file with the government saying all of their employees had finished this and that and were ready for this and that. I would also meet the new Warden who had taken over because the last Warden couldn't adequately handle the rash of "incidents" which had occurred at the prison such as the cell phone discovered in an inmate's cell that had a very good long distance plan and the guard who shot himself in the leg on perimeter patrol duty after being reassigned for having a liaison with a prisoner in the prisoner's cell for three hours; that warden had tendered his resignation.

I got there about 1:30 p.m. and went through the orientation, which was really stupid, and met the new Warden who had come here from a facility in Florida. The Warden was going to meet with all of the prisoner-students in the facility's education programs. I was ready to leave when he asked if there was anything I would need, and I said no that I thought everything was going really well. Then we heard a scratchy, uneven yet firm voice singing "One Day at a Time, Sweet Jesus." The warden turned and listened for a minute, then turned back to me and Ms Wilson with a perplexed look on his face.

"Oh, that's Crazy Eddie," I said, nodding my head and shrugging a little, "He eats garbage." Ms. Wilson nodded her head too.

As I left, I noticed that Special Kay was going into the classroom for the meeting with the Warden followed closely by Hand Job who had the biggest grin on his face and looked to be unbuttoning his pants.

On Saturday, I was at Caleb's next-to-last football game, and I was already in a very bad mood because I'd gotten there at 9 a.m. because Caleb told me to be there at 9 a.m.; then, I got there and found out his team wasn't playing until 11:30. Caleb just wanted to get there early so he could "practice" even though none of his teammates or even his coach showed up until 10:30 a.m.

It didn't help that I had been up late trying to talk the sheriff's department into coming and picking up the emu that appeared to be nesting in the woods behind our house as well as flirting with Cat. I found out from the sheriff's department that basically we had a new pet; the kids said they were going to call her Gracie.

Anyhow, Caleb played for the Midgets (which started at 11:30 a.m.) and the Peewees (which started at 1 p.m.). If I understood the coaches correctly, the players were somehow divided by age, weight, and astrological sign. Caleb was good enough to play for both. I don't know where he got his athletic ability from.

Allie cheered for the Midget team, making this an all day family affair.

Saturdays used to be such fun. I'd sleep late and get up and eat at a leisurely pace while watching my favorite cartoons. Not now. On this particular day, I observed a mother and son leave the bleachers, walk out of the fence and smoke. The mother actually gave her son, who could not be older than fourteen, a cigarette and lit it for him. Maybe I shouldn't have been surprised, but I was. And I was angry. How could a mother or father do something they know will cause damage to a child? Caleb will have to take two pills (maybe more later) every day for life. Because of drinking. Addiction was the only thing his mother, Lynn, was successful at. Somehow it filled a vessel so deprived of self esteem as to be a mere shell. And when Caleb entered that vessel, he had to compete with the alcohol. Caleb is a beautiful child who excels in sports and does semi-sort-of-okay in school work. But the alcohol won. It left its mark in the Concerta and Cyproheptadine that he must take every day. Last week while he was taking the pills, he looked at me and said, "When will I be okay?" I didn't have an answer.

On Sunday, Allie went to church with a friend's family. Diane went to church with Sara and Mckenna. I went out to my car to get some papers out that I had to grade when the church van came to get Caleb. The youth minister got out, shook my hand and introduced himself while we were waiting for Caleb to come out. Then he looked down towards Cat's pen and said, pointing down the yard, "Hey, you know you got emus?"

I went back to bed.

26

I would have liked to have a real psychotic break, but I couldn't; I guess I am too grounded in reality. But sometimes reality is just too real. Out at the prison this past week, I discovered that they no longer just housed inmates who were slightly off kilter; now they were open to other anti-social psychopaths as well. This would explain why one of the guards was taken prisoner for a while on Tuesday which was the day I was out there. The kidnapping happened after I left, but it did give pause for thought and questions to ponder, such as, "Why am I out here?" and "Are they paying me enough?"

Another one of my students, whom I call Goo Goo Eyes, was in love with me. He could just be doped up, it was difficult to tell sometimes. He just sat in class making these big moon eyes in my direction and occasionally winking, which I grant you seemed pretty cut and dried, but I was just not up on the finer points of prison etiquette. He might have been telling me that he liked my teaching style. Maybe I should try to fix him up with Hand Job.

Special Kay, at his psychotic best, came into class fussing and yelling about discrimination and conspiracies. I had just asked the class which term was more appropriate, Black or African American, so I asked him which one he preferred to be called, thinking it might distract him from his tirade.

He yelled, "I'm a psycho-American, and we're gonna take over the world."

The man sitting next to him snorted and said, "Yeah, we're the Thorazine Warriors; tremble in fear." I did get a kick out of this class.

Then Special Kay said he wouldn't be my student much longer because he was growing a horn and would be a unicorn in a couple of weeks. He really did have a boney ridge in the middle of his forehead. I really like mythological beasts, so I told him I'd visit. Plus, we were going to be finished with class in a couple of weeks so him being a unicorn shouldn't hurt my retention rate. Then Special Kay smiled and said it was good luck to rub a unicorn's horn.

I really needed to get more mileage to come out here.

My mother had shoulder surgery and, as with the carpal tunnel surgery, had waited almost too long. This was just the latest in the continuing deterioration of her body. Grandma and Grandpa wanted to be there, but they were both not feeling well. Sara couldn't get off of work, but she and Mckenna had come by the house to stay until the kids got dressed for school and then took them to the bus stop. As Mamma and I left, they'd hugged her three or four times each and the "Bye, you're my baby, you're my baby doll, you're my best friend, bye I love you" had gone on for at least twenty minutes. I got her to the hospital early, and Mamma went into the bathroom of the hospital room to put on the flimsy hospital gown. The nurse came in to give her something to make her sleep. We waited for it to take effect, not speaking.

She finally went to sleep, and I sat there in a chair in front of the window watching her breathe. Rise. Fall. Peaceful. Chemical peace. A momentary break from the pain. Up. Pause. Down. There was absolutely nothing in my head. I couldn't form a thought. The book I'd brought to help pass the time sat unused and lonely on the table.

I got up and went to the rail of her bed, looked into that once-beautiful face and whispered, "You're my best friend. Don't you die on me. I can't do this by myself." My secret fear. Being all alone with five kids. Or just being all alone. No counter-balance for my phobias, stupidity or anger.

Two white-clad gentlemen came in and wheeled her to surgery. I don't think I exhaled until she came back two hours later.

Yesterday, I took my mother back for her follow-up appointment.

I know Mamma was in pain, but she had gotten really good at concealing it. The fibromyalgia and her shoulder problem had started with a tingling in her shoulder and a loss of feeling in her arms. We had to hurry because we had to be back home in time to pick the kids up from the bus stop.

We got to the clinic and were immediately put in one of those little rooms. Then an overly officious nurse came in and started showing my mother the exercises that she would have to start doing. My mother thought this was most amusing since she couldn't move her shoulder and arm at all without intense pain. In fact, when the nurse insisted on demonstrating some of the exercises on my mother, my mother winced, said two cuss words, and then said to the nurse in an amazingly normal tone of voice, "If you do that again, I swear I will kill you and everyone you love." Impressive.

27

I hate sports. Of any kind. Football. Baseball. Wrestling. Hockey. Swimming. Gymnastics. Wait. Not the last two, or at least not the men's divisions of the last two. I hate going to practice. I hate going to games. I hate sitting in the bleachers. I hate walking across the grass to get to the bleachers.

As I was driving to school this morning, I noticed that Caleb had left his practice football in the front passenger's seat and that Allie had left her pompoms in the back seat. I knew that this was God's divine retribution for me not ever going to any sporting event as a child, as an adolescent, or as a young adult. I didn't even watch them on television. Who knew that every child in my house would think he or she is a sporting sensation? Although based on my present savings' rate, my best retirement plan might be to get them in a major league of some sort.

Caleb would come into the house and say that he had bludgeoned someone to a bloody pulp on the field, and I was supposed to say, "You get 'em kid!!" It just didn't seem right. Allie was telling me the other day that no one was talking to this one girl on the squad because she didn't have the "right" kind of bloomers. I'm not sure that I agree with what this stuff was supposed to be teaching (nor did I understand what it was supposed to be teaching).

Caleb's last game was at Northeast High School at 11 a.m. I had to get up early on Saturday and drive him and Allie all the way across town to the match. I took an umbrella, seventy sunscreen, and a book.

I surveyed the field looking for any signs of shade. Then I saw it at the far end of the field. That was where I plunked down for the duration. Reading my book. Every once in a while I looked up to see if my kid was running the ball or cheering. If they were, I would let out a gentle "Go Allie/Caleb" (complete with raised hand for added emphasis) and continue reading. The other parents would pass (I was located on the path to the restrooms) and look me as if I had antennae on my head. How could anyone not enjoy the "sport of champions"; I wonder if the parents of Sumo wrestlers have the same philosophy: "Oh Hichiko! One day you will be fatter than anyone, and you'll push them out of the circle in two seconds while looking very good in your bathing thong!" I sat there and listened to these parents gently yell things like "Kill him!!" or "Don't you let him get through or I'll stomp you in the ground!" This last was from a delightful Goth couple- for some reason I christened them the Joneses- who had very black hair, very black clothes and very white skin – albino white- adorned with lots of tattoos and piercings. Probably Republican too.

Then came a grandmother named Granny Addie who was obviously there to hurl insults at her grandson. She came up to me and said pointedly, "Who've you got out there?" I told her and she said, "He's pretty good. I'll bet he'll put someone in the hospital."

I looked at her and said, "I hope not."

She looked at me like I was a pedophile and then she looked at my book (which had really gotten interesting in the last few pages) and she said, "What are you doing?" I told her that I really didn't care for football, and I was just here for the kids. Granny Addie asked, "Ain't you a Christian?"

"No," I said, "but I can simulate."

That threw her. Maybe I was a snob. I liked the kids to be involved, but I just wished it didn't have to be quite so violent. Or time consuming. Or boring. But then where else would I meet Granny Addie and the Joneses? Caleb scored three touchdowns; his team won. Which meant we were in the playoffs. In the beautiful town of Sebastopol, a wonderful forest-and-armadillo-filled drive into the middle of nowhere.

28

I got to take Allie and three of her friends to dinner and a movie in celebration of Allie's birthday. I couldn't say that I was looking forward to this, but my mother was still recuperating and couldn't do it so I was in the fallback position. Plus I thought I might need to spend some more time with Allie.

Last week, I had been greeted at the door when I got home from work by my mother saying, "You need to talk to Allie." Mamma then handed me an effigy that she'd found in Allie's room. It looked remarkably like Caleb. Allie is very artistic. She'd even stuck pins in it. When I asked her about it, she said that Caleb had been mean to her. She had also heard me talking to Mamma about making effigies at work. Kids pick up everything, even when they don't seem to be listening.

At work, my office was across the hall from a very good friend of mine, Jane. We had known each other for many years. Once when I was visiting New Orleans, I got a voodoo kit and, when I got back, she and I would take turns pretending the voodoo dolls were people we "had a bit of trouble with" and stick pins in them. Obtaining a personal possession from the person added a whole other level of satisfaction. You wouldn't believe how much stress this relieved! When either one of us was having a bad day, we'd call the other on the phone and say, "Meet me in the office!" Then, we'd proceed to kill or maim or just torture those who did their psychological worst to us.

Then we had to stop. Her secretary - an extremely religious woman who, with just a bit of imagination I could see barefoot in a tattered dress handing out snakes and saying, "If you believe in the Holy Spirit, nothing will happen!"- just did not see the humor in voodoo and felt that we would be going immediately to Hell unless there was substantial divine intervention. She would leave religious paraphernalia on Jane's desk. As we were in the buckle of the Bible belt (and both of us really needed our jobs), we decided that cooler heads must prevail. But it was fun for a while. Her secretary, who reminded me of my grandmother, left shortly after that because she could make more money working two days a week at a doctor's office than she could working full time for the college.

Jane left too. After working here for fourteen years. She left for two very specific reasons. The first was that she's lesbian and her partner of eighteen years wanted to take a class from us. It's common practice for the classes of husbands, wives, children (even nieces and nephews and grandparents and girlfriends of some higher-ups but we low individuals on the totem pole are not supposed to know about that) to be paid for by the school. When Jane asked them to pay for her partner's class, the administration said no. And they told her that she could take legal action if she so chose, but that Mississippi law was very clear on the subject; we rainbow-colored people had no rights.

The second reason she left was because of the reaction she got when Jane and her partner decided to have a commitment ceremony. Jane's parents let them have it in their house and even catered the event. Jane sent out invitations and (thoughtfully, I thought) included the people in her division. Those people (many of whom she'd been working with since she'd started here) turned on her. Refusing to attend this "abomination." Even asking how she could be so casual about something so "unnatural." The Dean of Student Services himself told Jane that "he and his wife would not be attending because it went against their personal beliefs and was an affront to God." I bet he was going back to the sauna instead.

29

My prison class was about to end, and most of the students were doing very well. Special Kay wrote an excellent paper from Lockdown (he was back in); I had to take the final to him there. I got a lot of compliments from the other prisoners in there who wanted me to "teach" them something (though I was pretty sure it wasn't language related) and one gentleman who wanted me to be his "luv monkey." Hand Job and Goo Goo eyes were still very much in love with each other, and I couldn't help but feel somewhat responsible. One of the prisoners failed; I had been worried about any failures in that class and had already decided to curve the grades based on the prisoners' release dates although it wasn't ethical (but it was imminently practical). The prisoners turned out to be some of the best students I'd ever taught. The last time he was in class, Special Kay got very upset about the fact that he wasn't a unicorn yet and that the horn in the middle of his forehead had stopped growing. He even asked if I thought that taking that stuff that makes penises grow bigger would help. He usually carried on two conversations with two different people neither of whom were in evidence (they were in his head), but he always politely whispered to them. I empathized as much as I could before we got to work on our assignment.

The one dark cloud in the class was a student called T-bone. After I had assigned the essay, he went on a rant. "You discriminatin!!" he shouted at me. "You tryin to take away our language!" "You tryin to make us speak right!" According to him, there was a (presumably) white conspiracy that I was a part of which was trying to, as he said, "Take the black out of black folks."

Now this is the same student who on the last paper said that he really wanted an A; I said that he should work hard, do his very best and we'll see. He said, "No, you don't understand. I REALLY want an A." I just brushed it off, but when he turned in his paper, there was a note attached that said, *"Mr. Stewart, I really want an A on this paper, and I thought you should know that I'm in here for murder."* He got a B. His tirade followed his confession that he didn't think he had any brain cells left because he'd "smoked a little too much a' what he shoulda been sellin'."

I was usually so calm in the face of student rampages, but this rant pissed me off royally. I yelled that he was just saying all of that because he didn't want to do the essay, and he wanted to throw up as much dirt as possible. I also told him that if he thought that I discriminated, he was more than welcome to file a complaint and leave the class and go right back to his cell. *Headline: Teacher Stabbed at Lost Gap; Mouth to Blame!* I think I shocked T-bone. I know I shocked Special Kay (and his invisible friends), Hand Job, and Goo Goo Eyes. Henderson even stopped in the class and asked if everything was okay. I calmed down, told Henderson everything was fine, and then told the class to get to work, eyeing T-bone as I said this. They got to work and didn't say anything else. At the end of class, the students filed out, turning in their essays as they left. T-bone was last. He waited until everyone had left and the door was closed; then he said, "If I had had a teacher like you when I was in high school, I might not be in here now." And he turned in his essay.

30

I took my minivan to have a tire repaired. I called it my minivan even though my mother drove it everywhere. It should have been hers, but when "we" went to the car place, "we" discovered that my credit was so much better than hers; hence, it was mine. Joy. So I was absolutely positive that I would end up buying a new tire and was *thrilled* by the prospect. I was there barely two seconds, and they came back in and said, "The car is ready, Mr. Stewart." And not only that, it was not going to cost anything. I was *ecstatic*! Lalalalalala. There was nothing wrong with the tire! I should have stopped there but no; being the glutton for punishment that I was (five kids, remember), I decided to take my Camry down to have the tires rotated and aligned and balanced. It was supposed to cost $55.79; it had to be done as the holidays were coming up and I always ended up doing a lot of transporting various children hither and thither. I hadn't been there ten minutes before the man said, "You're going to need new tires, Mr. Stewart."

"All four at once?" I asked in a bit of a squeaky voice.

"Yes," he replied in the manner reserved entirely for mechanics when they are talking to foolish laypeople.

So I asked the next logical question, "How much will it cost?"

He hemmed and hawed and (pretended, I think) to look at some books and make estimates on a calculator then looked at me and said (with a straight face no less) "$310." At the best of times, I couldn't come up with $100 much less $310, and we were just beginning the Christmas season. There was no way. So I said, "There's no way!"

He then showed me how much I needed the new tires which entailed walking around the car – like we're playing "London Bridge" – and touching each of the tires; he said we could try for a new credit card. So within five minutes, I had a new credit card with a $1600 limit at an amazing 16% interest rate. How could I possibly lose?

They took my car and hauled it onto the lift and proceeded to put the new tires on. Shortly after that, this same man came back in and said, "I need to show you something, Garland." He was now calling me "Garland" because we were about to have sex ; the $310 was just foreplay.

He took me outside, pointed to the backend of the car and said (I swear), "The frumbaling manifold tweaks astir Lord Cromwell."

I just nodded my head and grinned like a fool because I had no idea what was going on but was pretty sure it would cost me. This "frumbaling" thingy had to be replaced and would cost approximately $1,100. I was thrilled. And said so. Pointedly. But to no avail. This wondrous credit card that had magically dropped in my lap was soon maxed out; I got the car back late that afternoon. Jasper (yes, I called the mechanic by his first name because we had been intimate in the way that could only be accomplished by the people who have you over a barrel) was as nice as could be.

I don't know why I'm complaining; the car was ten years old, had two hundred thousand miles on it, was in need of a paint job, but didn't have any car payments; changing the frumbaling made it drive better than it had in years. Who needed Christmas presents anyway? I again said the words which had become my mantra: "Maybe next year would be better." Maybe.

31

My sister Lynn, for some reason, was absolutely positive that I had money. Lots of it. She called the other day to ask me to give her first husband (Trisha's father) $13,000 so he wouldn't lose his land so that, after he dies, "Trisha would have something to remember him by." I told her that I couldn't come up with that much if my life depended on it, and I was still trying to come up with $1,600 to pay off my new credit card. She hung up.

Then she called yesterday to see if Mamma and I would take Joey's (husband three's) six month old baby (by his latest crack addict) and raise it. My emotions were in extreme turmoil and became knotted up in my stomach and were able to be expressed only through cussing. So I cussed. A lot. My response boiled down to: "Who the (insert offensive word) do you (insert offensive word)ing think you are? I'm trying to raise YOUR kids. What makes you think that I would raise anyone else's, especially that little (male organ) (anal orifice) who beat you up every other day?" Something about cussing just brings out the innate creativity in me. Probably because I was taught that it is wrong and will cause me to burn in Hell, so I figured if I could make it witty that God would overlook the use of invective.

I didn't understand how my sister's heart could go out to any children except her own. Children adored her, all children. I've seen her offer to baby sit the children of people she had just met, sometimes for weeks at a time. But not her own. What happened to her nurturing instinct? She probably smoked it. In a pipe.

Sometimes I wondered if there was a defining moment that a person could look at and say, "That's where it started to go bad." I know that everyone plays the "if only" game (and I'm the world's worst) but there were times when I looked around myself and asked "When did this happen?" "When did it get this bad?" I think a person's self esteem and determination and, yes, even intelligence, don't disappear in one fell swoop, they are eroded away in small increments. Slowly. Over time. Marked by each little decision made down a certain path.

Lynn was always the most conscientious and the funniest and the undisputed center of attention. And the most disturbed. She was my mother's favorite as well as my grandmother's and grandfather's. Then she started drinking and gate-wayed herself to where she is now.

I tried to feel sorry for her; I tried to feel anything for her, but I couldn't.

I took Mamma to see Lynn a few days before the Christmas holidays began. I hadn't seen her in a long while and didn't want to see her now. But Mamma couldn't drive, so I drove up the pockmarked driveway to the trailer whose only source of heat is a small wood burning stove in the (alleged) living room. I sat in the car while Mamma knocked on the door, but there was no answer. Chris (her present fling) was no where to be found. He drank and did other things as badly as she did; he was probably dumpster diving for cans and other recyclables to sell.

Mamma pushed the door open and went inside. I waited. And waited. And waited. Then, exasperated and more than ready to go home, I went to the door and walked in. The trailer was immaculate except for what looked like dried blood on the worn carpet. You could have eaten off of the vinyl floor. Lynn always was a good housekeeper. Even her shoes and, I'm guessing, Chris' were set neatly by the wall. Over the shoes, and in almost the center of the dried blood spray, was a hole in the wall. Head sized.

Lynn was sleeping on the couch. Since I'm six years older than her and because her father left so soon after she and Sara were born, I had always been more of a father figure to her than a brother. I remembered her wearing my mother's bra to school when she was in the second grade and stuffing it with socks. I remembered her breaking her foot at the skating rink and not wanting to leave until it closed because she'd "paid to stay until eleven." I remembered her giving birth to Trisha when the world (and she) was young and full of possibilities. I saw her thin chest rising and falling with each breath. There was a large knot on her forehead, both her eyes were black, and her nose didn't look exactly like it should have. There were cuts on her cheeks and neck. Head wounds bleed a lot. Mamma was sitting beside her, holding her hand, crying. The penitent who didn't know what sin she'd committed seeking a forgiveness that would not come. I sat on the couch and put my head on Mamma's good shoulder. We sat there a long time. The Penitent, the Sinner, and the Seeker, looking for answers, absolution, and acceptance. Just another in a multitude of unholy trinities. Lynn just kept sleeping and never knew we had been there.

32

My alarm went off at 4:00 a.m. You must understand the depth of my sacrifice since my alarm didn't even go off at 4:00 a.m. when I was working and *never* during a holiday, much less Christmas holiday. But here it was 4 o'clock in the morning.

My awaking at this hour was due to my innate sense of guilt and lack of self esteem. And due to the convoluted nature of my family, so of course I blamed them. My mother was adopted by my grandparents when she was seven. She remained in contact with her father (who we called Pop) and one of her sisters, Auggie Belle (pronounced "Awg-y-bell-a" and don't forget the final "a"). Her other natural brothers and sisters were enjoying the fresh air and vigorous exercise provided by some Texas Correctional Facility or other. Pop died a few years ago, so now we only see Auggie. Twice a year. And this year she came with her oldest son, BB.

BB was forty-four years old, and if he has another name I've never heard it. BB also was an avid hunter who wanted to kill something in Mississippi. He just loved to talk and spend time in the bathroom trying to overload the capacity of both the toilet and the septic tank. Even the bathroom fan seemed to struggle. He just had surgery for hemorrhoids a few weeks before his visit and was supposed to take it easy, but he wasn't going to let something as insignificant as hemorrhoids prevent him from making a kill in the Magnolia state. Every time I passed by the bathroom while he was in it, I could hear moans and groans and

117

the requisite cussing that the bathroom fan couldn't quite cover up. He said that taking a shit felt like "trying to pull barbed wire out my ass."

On this particular morning, BB wanted to go hunting and was afraid my "rinky dink piss poor" alarm wouldn't wake him up (as I had said that I would be more than happy to put it next to his bed). So I put it next to my bed, set it and, when it rang, got up to get him up.

The rest is even harder to believe. I got dressed to go hunting. From the depths of my soul, I hate hunting. My grandfather used to attempt to take me hunting. The last time was when I was ten; we went squirrel hunting. At least I think that was what we were looking for.

We walked into the middle of the woods and my grandfather said, "You wait here. I'll circle around and drive them this way."

"I have a better idea," I said. "Why don't I just go with you and we'll chase them until they get really tired."

He just looked at me for a long minute, said, "I'll be back soon" and left.

I waited, quite patiently for the first fifteen seconds, then I got a bit disturbed. I heard tree branches breaking and thought it had to be a bear. I saw birds overhead and just knew they were buzzards there to feed. I heard the leaves crackling and thought snakes were coming my way. I didn't even think about cocking the gun in my hands. Great White Hunter. That was me.

And that had been at least twenty eight years before, when I was in a better mood.

So why was I doing this? Well, the short of it was it was my mother's fault. She said (and I quote), "I think it would be nice if all of the guys would go hunting and bring back a big ol' deer."

I actually said, "I beg your pardon" because I didn't think I'd heard that woman right. I still maintain that she was just getting me back for telling her to flash a boob at the washing machine repairman because I thought it might get us a discount. Plus the look on her face had been priceless. As soon as she said this, every human in the house took up the refrain, "Unk's going hunting." BB, Auggie Belle, Mom, Caleb, Allie, and Diane. I finally agreed to go simply to shut them up. So I got up at the crack of butt early in the morning, put on two pairs of pants, two pairs of socks, and three shirts. Then I put on my jacket (the only jacket I have) and sat down to drink coffee while BB and Caleb got ready.

It was cold outside. We were going hunting at my grandfather's place, and I would have had to show BB how to get there anyway (BB never got lost; he just became, as he said, "bewildered"). So I pulled up in my Camry with BB following in his truck, with his 4 wheeler on the back. We got out; all of us were packing; they had guns, I had my wits. We commenced trekking in the woods; BB and Caleb were kind enough to let me bring up the rear, and I was happy to oblige.

We hadn't gotten far into the woods at all when they stopped and almost as one turned around to face me; then BB said, and I quote, "Your coat is too loud." So I had to take it off and put it in the car.

When I caught back up with them, they were at the deer stand. Now I was just being polite. It was really deer public housing. And there was only room for two of us at a time, three if no breathing was involved. BB claimed he had to be in the deer stand, so he could make his kill. It was heated, but he assured me that had nothing to do with him wanting to be in it. Caleb and I got to rotate in about every twenty minutes. I also got to shiver and turn blue (Did I mention it was cold?).

And then I became acquainted with another feature of hunting. The silence. I didn't seem to remember this part from when I hunted with my grandfather, which may be the reason he was so thrilled to drop me from his hunting regimen. Hunters have to be quiet. Most people who know me know that I have a predisposition to banter, and I consider it one of my strong points. This is definitely not appreciated in hunting circles. BB actually told me to shut up when I asked after at least eight minutes of absolute silence, "So, what's up?" They just glared at me.

Then I said I had to go to the bathroom. I was told in no uncertain terms that I could not go anywhere around the public housing because it would drive off the deer. So I had to walk by myself over the hill away from the deer stand and the rifles. Very far away as I didn't want any accidents of any kind. That was when I had a very surreal moment (everything up to this point had been too real). There I was in the absolute silence of the woods using the restroom (there's just something exhilarating about peeing in the wild) when what should appear but a rather large deer that the "bewildered" hunter had just told me that my urine would drive it off. That didn't seem to be happening. If anything, this deer was coming closer.

For some reason, it reminded me of a morning in Saudi Arabia. It was about the same time of the morning, and I had gotten up to go jogging. This was the second time I had been jogging in Saudi. The first time I had gone jogging, I was arrested because the religious police in that very small village just didn't know what to make of an extremely white man running along the street at that hour of the morning. They asked me for my papers – foreigners are supposed to keep papers on them at all times - and I didn't have any papers – because I was running – and they were not amused. They took me to the station. Curiously, in Saudi Arabia, you don't get a phone call, you just kind of wait around until somebody misses you. I waited three hours. The police officers were real cool about it and kept giving me a thumb's up gesture and saying the only English word they knew – "okay." They also gave me a lot of really sweet tea to drink.

Anyway, my second time out jogging, I was running down the street when I kept hearing a "clop, clop, clop" sound. I stopped and continued to hear the sound; in fact, it got louder. Then I saw a donkey, running down the road with a piece of a rope still around its neck. It was getting the hell out of Dodge. I couldn't help but laugh because I knew that no one would ever believe me if I told them. That's how I felt when I saw the deer. I realized that I just couldn't let this deer be murdered, and it was headed in the general direction of my deranged family. So I whispered loudly, "Get out of here" and gestured vehemently. It just looked at me and calmly kept grazing. So I picked up a large rock and threw it and continued the vigorous arm movements. The deer got the hint and ran away.

I turned and saw BB and Caleb staring at me. They had decided to "answer the call of nature" and find out what was taking me so long. They looked at me, looked at the deer track, and BB (who up until this time was on his way to being my favorite cousin) said, "I think we can take it from here," and I was banished.

I got home and ran immediately to my bed, covered up, and cranked up the electric blanket. I looked at my clock and it read, *"5:45 a.m."*

Our guests finally went home after about 5 days. Of course it wasn't all bad. I got to see my Grandmother turn purple when she asked BB if he had a girlfriend and he said that he didn't and that he had used his right hand so much that "he felt he should buy it a present." Couth is so overrated, and some moments are priceless. It was really good to have company occasionally, but it was even better to see them leave. After three days, no one is a guest anymore.

33

The first, second, and third days of classes went very well. I had a couple of students cry (mainly nerves- they return to school after being out a number of years and they aren't ready for it emotionally), but I metaphorically held their hands, and they were okay. The fourth day proved especially interesting. I thought that because I wasn't at the prison this semester that I wouldn't have any interesting (substitute the word "crazy" here) students. I was wrong.

I had one elderly gentleman in my class who was very quiet and seemed to be a very nice man. Then class ended and we happened to walk up to the main building together, with me talking to him and trying to make him feel welcome. I found out he'd been out of school for forty years and was back trying to get a degree in Communications. I complimented him on his intestinal fortitude and said that I was impressed that he'd decided to do this at this time in his life.

Then he said, somewhat doggedly, "I just got to get a degree in Communication. I got to find the bug the government put in me."

My mind hiccupped; I said, "Hunh?"

He looked at me warily, leaned closer and continued, "They put it in me some-odd 30 years ago. And I just can't find the damned thing." He pulled his backpack back up on his shoulder and said, "But I'll be damned if they get the better of me. I'm gonna show those Yankees!"

He had decided after much deliberation on a two-pronged attack. He would learn all there was to know about bugs, and he would sue the government. He was acting as his own attorney and "he was gonna get more money than the national debt." Then he asked me if I'd ever heard him on the radio.

"I'm pretty certain that I haven't," I said, looking around for witnesses.

"Not all things is bad, I guess. This damned bug lets people hear my thoughts."

"Anybody?" I asked, not letting go like I should have.

"No, just when I'm thinking a certain way," he said, "But if I'm thinking that way and you are standing near a computer or a television or a radio, you can hear me."

"Oh," I said, and stopped, having no idea what else to say.

"You know they call me Brother God," he confided, pulling his back pack up again.

"Who does?" I asked.

"The people who hear me. They don't know where the voice comes from, so they call me Brother God."

I sighed. He had seemed like such a nice man. And he really was. He was just interesting. I made a beeline to a friend of mine's office because she works in the Special Populations office and gets to deal with students like him all of the time; she had no record of him. I assured her that I was fairly certain that more than one person lived in that skull, and she "tskk tskked" me.

The next time I saw him he asked me to read over the transcript of the trial, and he pulled out a stack of papers that contained meaningless gibberish. I dutifully took it, and "filed" it in the trash can. Then he told me about the engine he'd built that didn't need gasoline that the government was keeping under wraps "until the trouble in Iraq is over." He asked if I'd seen some speech the president had given. I said, "No." He then laughed, slapped his thigh, and said he really got the government that time. All during the speech he kept interrupting (using his Brother God ability) by singing and saying things like "Let's kill the President." I convinced him to go see my friend in Special Populations. She talked to him for at least a couple of hours and issued her expert opinion: "Yep, he's crazy." What to do. What to do. I missed Special Kay.

34

It was time that I admitted a horrible fact that could be avoided no longer: I was fat. I had gone from a thirty-two inch waist to a thirty-four inch waist to the point where I didn't really want to know. I went through my closet and started trying on some of my old clothes. Now I assumed that they would fit because I'd been diligently or maybe semi-diligently, make that quasi-diligently, working out. There was this one particular pair of pants that I recall loving about eight years ago. I put them on, and everything seemed to be going well until I looked in the mirror. Those pants were not happy. Every seam was ready to burst. Then I tried to put my hand in the pocket and found that I couldn't get it in there without lubricant. I got to thinking about my family genetics, so I got on some scales. I weighed two hundred and thirty five pounds at what is essentially one Earth gravity. I was a fat muffin and not as handsome as I thought or pretended that I was. Damn. Mamma said she felt exactly the same way when almost overnight according to her, she went from looking "hot" to looking "good for her age." And she never got over it.

In addition to being fat, I was old. The first was unforgivable in the gay world; the second makes you a pariah, and no amount of working out helps. There are just three ages for a gay man: twink, tomcat, and troll. I was in that awkward in-between phase, not quite a dirty old man but getting there rapidly. And having young, wrinkle-free students didn't help. My office was located at the intersection of two very busy hallways in the main building on our campus. This meant that I was privy to a lot of conversations that students were having, and it helped me keep my finger on the pulse of what was happening which I think makes me sound a lot cooler than I actually was.

One day, I was sitting at my desk and heard a conversation that four young ladies were having outside of my office. They were talking about an instructor who is relatively new to our campus. They were talking about how "fine" he was and saying things like "I'd like a piece of that" and such and the longer I sat there, the madder I got. When I finally had had enough, I got up and stuck my head out of my office and said, "Pardon me, but I don't think you realize that I can hear everything you say, and I just had to tell you how offended I am."

One young black lady with dreadlocks said, "I'm so sorry. I didn't know that there was an office there." And she made a vague gesture in the general direction of my office.

But I was in no way finished; I continued, "Do you realize how inconsiderate it is to talk about how hot that teacher is and not mention me at all? I've been working out until I think my ass will fall off, and no one calls me 'muffin' or uses any other endearment." My righteous indignation had reached a fevered pitch, but I couldn't keep it up so I smiled at them.

Dreadlock girl smiled and asked, "Who are you anyway?" So I told her and they walked away still laughing. You really must stand up for yourself, or no one else will.

After class, I was asked to speak to the Health and Occupational Student Association (they go by HOSA) by one of the Health and Occupational Educators the following Saturday. Since they used HOSA for the name of the organization, I thought it would be funny if they called themselves the HOE's. They didn't find that funny in the least which might be the reason that I've never been asked to speak to them again. They wanted me to speak about procrastination, and then they wanted me to give them a title for my speech. I thought long and hard about it but couldn't come up with a serious enough title to suit the HOSA-ites ;I kept emailing titles like "Hey, Let's Do This Later" or "Reincarnate the Problem" until they took the title-making job away from me and entitled my speech "Success In Small Doses" which I thought was way too grown up for me.

I arrived at the college Saturday and noticed millions of buses from all over the state and all of these extremely young people milling about. And they were all dressed up, in suits and ties or tasteful dresses.

Now let me say that I would only wear a suit if someone whom I really liked had died. My typical attire involved jeans. On this special day, I chose to wear slacks and a sweater. But it never fails; two seconds after I put nice clothes on it looks like I slept in them. Well, I did my lecture and had a great time. I was supposed to talk thirty minutes, but I really got into my subject and talked at least forty-five minutes. Afterwards, I was standing outside with Vice President Ryan, a dean, and two division chairs. They were complimenting me on my lecture, and I was feeling pretty full of myself. Just then I heard someone behind me say, "That Mr. Stewart sure is one hot muffin!" and I turned my head just in time to see some dreadlocks going out the door. It really does pay to advertise. Now, if only that'd work with some cute guy. No, that might not be such a good idea.

35

Caleb wanted to play baseball. I was not against sports mind you, but at the beginning of the school year I asked him which sport he wanted to play, football or baseball. He chose football; mainly I'm sure because that's the sport that was being played at the moment. Then it was time for baseball, and he wanted to play, claiming that he wanted to be a coach one day and that his playing all of these sports would give him both experience and edge. And I said no. Not just because of the money, which is always a consideration, but mainly because of the time "someone" (insert my name here) must spend taking him to practice and to games, not to mention that in baseball the games are during the week so I might end up in Beulah Hubbard – a happening, small accretion of houses with no fast food to speak of- on Tuesday night at 10 p.m. and still have a forty minute drive home and showers and eating dinner and the like. Plus there was the little matter of his failure for the nine weeks. I just couldn't do it. Add to it the fact that Megan's competitive cheerleading career was costing us a butt load of money because of the dance and tumbling classes she had to take as well as the travel to exotic locales that we were graciously allowed to pay for. And Diane wanted to play softball too.

So I maintained from the get-go that Caleb couldn't play baseball. Then my mother got into the picture and told him he could and actually took him to the organizational meeting. The coaches were salivating all over themselves because Caleb is a good athlete. Caleb came home thrilled that he will play baseball and wondering when he's going to pick out his uniform (about a hundred dollars) and telling me that his registration fee was forty-five dollars.

I said, "Talk to your grandmother; I'm not involved in this."

And my mother didn't say anything. She didn't say, "I don't have the money," which I knew she didn't. She didn't say, "I'm sorry Caleb, you can't play this year." She said nothing, just stared off into space. But Caleb, as well as some very irate coaches, said that I was preventing him from playing; this meant that guess who got to play the evil character yet again.

I love my mother for her generous heart and her willingness to help any and everyone. I just wish she would think about things a bit more, and be a bit more selective. If I didn't watch her, she'd max out every credit card she had; just to get the kids things they didn't need. Or she wouldn't pay her bills. Or she'd write bad checks.

I was envious. She was the one they went to; she was the one who gave solace. I was the bad cop, the naysayer; I was the one who brutally refused to let them do things. I was the one who made sure they were in bed at a certain time, showered, with their clothes out for the next day. But that doesn't matter to kids, does it?

I have this fear of the kids growing up and never coming back and me being left all alone on the top of this damn hill. But I still made sure they were in bed and showered and had all of their clothes out. Because I had to. It was the right thing to do.

Then there are the other family curses. I didn't get the alcoholism or the drug addiction that Lynn got, but I have started feeling a tingling in my shoulders and a loss of feeling in my arms. Double Damn.

36

Megan started putting on weight. Actually quite a lot of it. The main reason was that she was put on the pill recently (to regulate her period) and the hormones seemed to be playing havoc with her metabolism (but her period was regulated). She wanted me to go and buy all of this diet food, so she could get back to her cheerleading weight and was furious with me because I didn't go buy her all of these Lean Cuisines or Jennie Craig meals.

This morning she got up just before I did so she could take a shower; I know this because there was no hot water for me when I wanted to take a shower. She came in the kitchen and made herself a large bowl of Sugar Coated Double Chocolate Whizbangs or whatever (but put fat free milk on them) and I said sweetly, "Honey, that's not the way to eat if you want to lose weight."

She replied snidely, "What else can I eat? You didn't get any rice puffs." Then she added, "At least I'm not as big as you."

At that moment I thought about throwing her Sugar Coated Double Chocolate Whizbangs outside to let Cat eat them, but I remembered that chocolate wasn't good for dogs; instead I cursed her with my Mamma's girth (I later took it back, but the damage was done), and I allowed it to roll off of my back because I still felt that I was a hot muffin.

At some point and I'm not exactly sure when, I started having this sneaking suspicion that Trisha just might possibly be having sex with Kyle (I have no clue where I got the name Wyatt). When they were here, they would go back to Trisha's room, or she would go over to his trailer (yes, he's living large) for long periods of time. I might have been forty, but I vaguely recalled being seventeen and knew that not many people were as hormonally challenged as I was. And my mother wasn't fazed by any of this because Trisha was already on the pill and had the requisite regulated period.

Mamma didn't seem to remember sitting just outside of my door on the occasions (well, one occasion) when I had someone of the opposite sex in my room. And then she rushed in breathlessly and said, "That's enough. Let's go in the living room and have cookies. You can graph later after she leaves."

I said to my mother within earshot of Trisha because that was how we transmitted information in my house, "God, I hope they're doing it right" meaning that I hoped that they are using birth control because I ain't doing the baby thing again and Trisha said, "I think we are; at least he's usually on top." I think I fainted. Then she laughed and just smiled and smiled, claiming she was joking. My sense of humor was coming back to bite me on the ass.

37

I had decided that this year was supposed to be different, at least financially speaking. We were going to get out (and stay out) of the hole. I always thought that people who used credit cards to pay for groceries and such were both ignorant and stupid. I would watch in absolute horror as people loaded items on the check out conveyor and then paid with a card that was probably charging them at least twenty-nine percent interest. That was then. That was when I had money and could afford to judge. But when I could no longer do that, when I came to a time of the month when there literally was no more money and no hope of legally getting any, when the kids would look at me with large eyes that seemed to ask why I couldn't take care of them, that's when I had to get out the card. And since I was using this card and knew I couldn't pay anyway, why not get as many groceries as I could and have a great month? Stupid, hunh? That's the thing about being in need. That's the thing about being ground down to nothing or at least feeling that way. And there's no greater sense of failure in the world than not being able to care for the ones you love. It's soul destroying. In my mind, I knew that I didn't make enough money and there were just too many kids and at least we had the essentials; in my heart I should have been a better provider, and I was a failure.

But that was ending this year. No more. I got my income tax money and paid off all three of my credit cards and actually was able to put three hundred dollars in my savings account, which for the past

131

few years had just been for show. Under no circumstances would I use those credit cards again. Cash only.

Then the washing machine went out. Mamma washes at least five loads a day. Having no washing machine wasn't pretty. I had to get one, and I had to get a good one. $598.63. Plus sixty dollars to deliver and set it up. Of course, I couldn't do it; I could conjugate verbs, but no one would pay sixty bucks for that unless maybe I was naked. Probably not.

Next, the last half of our two and a half baths went kaput. We'd always had trouble with the half bath in front. The previous owners had poured concrete over the sewage line running from that bathroom to the septic tank; we had the line re-dug around the back porch, but it had never worked right. The toilet in the middle bathroom hangs up when you flush it. There's a note on the top of the tank reminding everyone to stand there until it finishes filling up and the water stops running. The toilet in the last bathroom didn't even pretend to work; we had a bucket in the bathtub next to the toilet that we filled and used to flush it manually. No plumber would come out here for such a "minor job." My wonderful house, held together by duct tape, WD40, and fervent wishes. Today I hide, yesterday I hid, often I have hidden. Yep, conjugating those verbs sure helped around the house.

Finally, I hit a piece of tire in the road and hurt the underside of my car to the tune of $1,457. Insurance paid most of that, but I had to come up with the five hundred dollar deductible I had to have on my insurance so that I could afford my insurance. Damn. Naked conjugation sure was looking more and more lucrative.

"Garland," Mamma said, "we're stuck in Newton. The van started jerking real bad. So I just pulled over. I was afraid to go any more. Can you come and get us?"

I got up, got dressed, and left. Megan and Trisha were with Mamma. Caleb, Allie and Diane were asleep, so I just locked the back door and left. Newton is about a twenty minute drive from our house. I got there pretty quickly and saw them immediately, parked at the Subway. We got the prom dress they had just bought from the second hand dress place which was the reason they had gone to Newton in the first place, locked the mini-van and came home.

I tried to sleep. I tossed and turned and dozed. I knew I'd probably have to max out my credit card, and I'd have to wait 'til next year's tax time to pay it off. Again. That was if nothing else happened. For about a year. Right. I dozed a little more.

At some point in the night I dreamed that I was a stainless steel bumble bee. A sexless drone. Forever working for someone higher up who didn't care about me or my family or any thing else I might be concerned with. I was entrusted with guarding the hive, and all I had was a stinger that tingled and lost feeling and wasn't as sharp as it used to be; I woke up worried about myself.

Somehow I got up the next morning and got the kids up. Pandemonium ensued as it usually does. Trisha and Megan got in a fight, as only sisters can, over who should wear a pair of sleek red panties that I thought were too adult for either of them, but no one had asked me. My mother finally took the panties that each of them was claiming and threw them in the utility room on the dryer. Caleb basically dusted himself off and got dressed in his usual surly fashion while Allie and Diane got dressed with almost no fuss. Because my mother had no car, I had to take the kids to the bus stop. I didn't have time to iron my pants, so I threw them in the dryer, put them on, tucked my shirt in as I was putting on my shoes, reminded Mamma to call a tow truck and ushered the kids into the car.

We barely made the bus, but I was late for work and this would be the day that I'd told my student Sean that I'd meet him before class to help him with some English. Sean is in a wheelchair, loves to drink beer and loves black women with large butts; he is an absolute joy to teach, the kind of student that makes teaching fun; he'd come from a local community that didn't handle disabilities well, and he'd been in a wheel chair all of his life. Because he was in this wheelchair and had some difficulty speaking, he was always put in the "special needs" classes where, according to him, he "didn't learn shit." He finally got tired of it, quit that school in the tenth grade, came here to get his G.E.D., and stayed on to get a degree; he wants to be a graphics designer. There was nothing wrong with his mind.

I ran by my office and threw some things on my desk and booked it to my classroom. I got there, and Sean was waiting with his helper

Wendy. I was out of breath because I'd been running, so I just stood there breathing. Wendy was just standing there, eyes twinkling madly.

"What?" I said, very annoyed. She pointed, and I looked down at my gray pants that had a pair of sexy red underwear static clinging to them. I peeled them off and stuffed them into my pants thinking to just brazen it out.

Wendy looked at me and said sweetly, still straight faced, "Hot date tonight?"

I tried to laugh, and I guess did a pretty good job of it. She and Sean didn't seem to notice. I helped him some and listened as Wendy talked about her recent trip to Disney World with her kids and grandkids. We parted with her saying, "You should take your kids one day." I taught my first class and ran back to my office.

"Mamma? Did you call the tow truck?"

"I called Simmons. Do you know what that woman wanted to charge to tow the van? Two hundred dollars. I couldn't believe it. I told her I'd call around and call her back."

"We have to have it towed."

"I know. I just can't see paying that much."

"Call around. I'll call back in a little while." I made it to my next class a couple of minutes late and ran through the lesson. I made it back to my office and collapsed into a chair. The phone rang. "Hello?"

"They can't find the car," she said without preamble.

"What?"

"Ty's Towing was gonna get the van for seventy-five dollars. The guy just called me; he's in Newton, and the car's not there."

"Mamma?" It might have been a question or a curse; I wasn't sure.

"I'm gonna call the police and see if they towed it. I'll call you back in a while."

Buzz. Buzz. Good drone.

My office walls started suffocating me like a blanket. My heart started pounding, and I couldn't open my left eye completely; my lungs were in a straight jacket, and someone was behind me tightening it. Where was that empty feeling? I used to feel so damned empty. No, the emptiness started in the world around me and then twisted inside me like a corkscrew. I gave to my students; I gave to the kids until I felt that I had nothing left. I forgot to hold something back. No one warned me that I needed to hold something back. I didn't want to be here. I wanted to be at Disney World. I didn't want this to be my life. Something's got to count for something. I was tired of feeling like a failure. I was tired of being a mindless drone and working for nothing (that must be where that dream came from).

I was trying to get a grip on myself and had just sat down on the floor of my office when Dr. Dennis walked by. I plastered a grin on my face and tried my darnedest not to look insane, but I don't think it worked because she passed by again a few seconds later, this time walking very slowly. My heart was going at hyper-speed, and I started hyperventilating. I was getting so lightheaded that I thought I'd float away. Is this how Allie felt when she had a panic attack? I'd always told her to think of something else. I couldn't get any air and the more I tried, the less I seemed to get. Think of something else. Class. It was time for me to go to class. I had to go to class, so I put forth one all out effort to pull myself together and made my way across campus. I saw a lot of people and I waved but they thought I was saying hello and they just waved back when I was really trying to scream at them that I was drowning and needed a preserver. Humor. If the plane crashes into water, the seat may be used as a flotation device. Where was my seat? My flotation device wasn't flotationing, and my damn tray wouldn't lock in the upright position. Where was my Valium? That was not funny; it was stupid. I tried again to put on my mask of comedy, but it kept fraying at the edges and slipping. No duct tape. I was on the verge of stopping where I was, falling to my knees and crying like a baby because I had finally had enough. I had finally reached the end of myself. But if I started crying, I wouldn't stop, not for a long, long time.

I got to class, and the students looked at me. I couldn't say anything for a minute. And they just watched. Calmly. Needing me. Needing me to be a rock. Needing someone to put on a pedestal. Needing someone to provide security in their insecure lives. Somehow they saw more in me than was actually there. But all I had was me, or at least the outline of me. No filling. And all I could give was me. Here you go. Waste not. And I calmed down. And fit myself back into myself for them, just like I do for my kids.

The lesson was about depression and suicidal tendencies. I only fit two of the tendencies, so I was not suicidal; there was always one foot that refused to head into the firmament, but I'd be lying if I said the thought had never crossed my mind. I couldn't end my life because my grandmother would never forgive me. Neither would my insurance company. And I was needed. Then we got to talking about goals and how important they are to helping ward off depression and keeping a person on track. It occurred to me that I have no goals. I hadn't had any in a while now. I don't know why. I plodded from emergency to emergency and counted myself lucky to be intact which would count as a victory, wouldn't it? There might have been a few embers of hope left, but I had to work really hard to get them re-ignited. And some days I was just too tired to put forth the effort. All I had was my tingly, lifeless stainless steel stinger. Was this what happened to others, the ones who were so bitter now? Teaching made me forget about myself long enough to calm down and the only reminder of the attack was the mother of all headaches which I was glad to have because it meant I could feel something. When I got back to my office, I decided to write my goals; it was important to have some:

> I want the world to stop unraveling.
> I want to know I raised five good decent human beings.
> I want my mother not to be in pain.
> I want to not feel like a failure.
> I want my mother not to write bad checks.
> I want not to be bitter.
> I want my sister to stop using.
> I want to fall in love.
> I want peace (on earth or of mind or even of ass)
> I want … I want to breathe.

I finished work and ran home to get the Vehicle Identification Number of the minivan off of our insurance papers. Then I ran to the courthouse, so I could get the tag number (as we had put all of this information in the glove compartment of the van itself). It was about 3:45 p.m. when I finally made it to Newton. I first went to the Subway where the young man behind the counter said he remembered Mamma and the girls from the night before but who didn't think Subway had the van towed, then I went to the Chinese restaurant next door where they had no idea what I was talking about, then to the check cashing place next to that where the woman assured me that she left at 4:30 the afternoon before and didn't get there until 9:00 this morning and she'd never laid eyes on the vehicle. The only thing left to do was to go to the police. So I did.

I walked right in the Newton Police Department and said, "I'd like to report a stolen van." I was taken to a room and an officer took down all of my information including the tag number and the Vehicle Identification Number; I felt so proud that I had all of this handy.

Then another policeman came in and said, "Where was the van parked?" I told him. He turned to the other guy and said, "I bet the cameras at Quick Lube caught the theft." He turned back to me and said, all policeman-like, "Meet us over there."

My adrenaline was just a rushing. I got back to the Quick Lube, which was facing the parking lot of Subway, parked, and went in. The policemen had the manager at the television, looking at the video. "What time was it again?" he asked.

"I picked them up about 9:35 p.m. last night and the guy at the Subway said that the van wasn't there this morning." There. I had given even more evidence.

He started fooling with the equipment. "Is that it?"

"Yes," I said, my heart beat faster. I was about to find the low life scum that took my Mamma's minivan and bring them to justice. He fast forwarded it some more, and I watched a tow truck come and put the van on the back. On the side of the tow truck I saw the name "Simmons Towing."

I called and asked the nice lady at Simmons if the van was there. It was. I then said, "We told you we would call you back!"

"I know," she said, "but I already had a guy in Newton, so I told him just to bring it on in. Our mechanic thinks the problem is in the transmission."

I turned to the policeman and said, "I am so sorry."

"That's okay," he replied, "This is the first case we've solved in a while. Kinda neat."

I got home and sat down on the couch. Mamma was still laughing about my adventure and swearing up and down that she wasn't going to pay Simmons a dime. Then Caleb came and sat next to me.

"Here's my homework," he said, "Will you check it?"

"You going to turn it in?" I asked, hoping he learned from past mistakes.

"Yeah," then he said, still looking, "you're not going to send me away, are you?"

"Where would I send you baby?" I said, still feeling a headache throughout my body, "We're both gonna be right here." Probably forever. I looked at Mamma washing dishes, heard Trisha and Megan arguing over a pair of jeans, looked out the front window and saw Allie and Diane trying to put Cat on the trampoline; then, I started going over Caleb's fractions with him.

38

I watched the monitors. Heart, breathing. The I.V. snaked down from the nutrient-filled bag and into his deeply tanned, wrinkled skin, and attached there. Delivering not-poison in a carefully controlled drip, drip, drip. The immediate area around the needle on the inside of his arm was red, a cotton ball stuck underneath a band-aid, just above the indent of his elbow. That was the only vein that would work. Evidence of other test wells was all over the insides of both of his arms.

Grandpa had fallen; well, actually he was outside feeding the dog and probably (and, according to my grandmother, completely illicitly) chewing tobacco. When he came back in, the storm door fell off of its hinges and onto him, knocking him over a couple of loose cement blocks and onto the ground. He had a huge bruise on his head, and the doctors were worried that he might have broken a couple of ribs. At least that was what that white-coated, stethoscope wearing individual muttered when I finally cornered him. My cousin could have brought Grandpa to the hospital and had even offered, but Grandpa (with Grandma's full support) had insisted on waiting for me. That was nice but I kept telling him that if he was hurt badly enough, he should get to the hospital as fast as he could. Thank goodness I was able and near.

I somehow managed to get his half dazed very large form into my economy sized car; Grandma just stood off to the side after handing me his insurance cards, a list of his medications and telling me to tell the doctors that all he'd eaten all day was cornbread and greens which he wasn't supposed to eat and she'd warned him not to. We got to the hospital and into the emergency room and finally consulted a real doctor who put him to bed and ordered tests. Lots of tests. Grandpa had dozed off after the x rays and the search for a suitable vein.

Eighty-six. I often wondered if I'd make it to eighty-six. His movements were slower now. He'd get up from his chair very carefully, make sure he had his balance and then grab his walker and amble away. So different from the almost overpowering person I'd known most of my life. He was finishing the cycle, being cared for almost like an infant. Not long now, he kept saying. Not long before the trials of this world were over and everything would be peaceful in Glory.

Standing vigil at least until they let me take him home, I watched his darkened form. His chest rising slowly, then descending. The small plastic tube under his nose delivering the oxygen that his lungs couldn't get enough of. For so long, I hated him. I hated everything that he stood for. We barely acknowledged each other. I was self-important, and he was self-righteous. He had made me feel small, and I had made him invisible, along with his church, beginning my vacillation from atheism to agnosticism with bouts of devout belief thrown in for good measure. From the time I was seventeen. Really sixteen. That was when the first skirmish in our long war began:

It was late spring, and I had stayed home from school pretending to be sick for some reason I don't remember. I'd been on a health kick lately and had really been working out. I'd just showered and put on some jogging pants and a t-shirt when I decided to fry a couple of eggs for a late breakfast. I found the small cast iron skillet and had just gotten the can of no-calorie- just-like -butter cooking spray out of the cupboard when the doorbell rang. Our house had an open L-shaped floor plan with the kitchen in the crook of the L, the living room with a sofa and love seat at one end and a television, sofa and two easy chairs at the other. The front door had three small windows in it running diagonally, but I didn't bother to look out. I just opened the front door which was right next to the sofa and gazed upon two of the most beautiful men I'd ever seen asking if they could tell me about the Church of Jesus Christ of Latter-day Saints. I don't think I could have spelled my name if I'd tried. And breathing was suddenly difficult.

One was about five foot eight and had a kind of burnished red hair and light brown eyes. The other was a couple of inches taller, my height, with black hair and green eyes. They both looked all of eighteen, maybe twenty, and were freshly scrubbed to the point of shining. I'm sure that their luster is a figment of my imagination. I was sixteen and testosterone-filled-to-overflowing. I found enough oxygen to mumble, "Okay" and, looking at their feet because I didn't dare look them in the eyes, I opened the screen door for them to come in, motioned vaguely to the sofa and, after closing the door behind them, sat on the love seat at the end closest to them. Thinking back, I know I turned the most moon eyed face in the known universe in their direction. And they didn't laugh. I could feel my heart beat behind my eyes. Every nerve in my body was erect when I managed to say the only thing I could think of which also happened to be one of the stupidest, "Are you really Mormons?"

The shorter one assured me that they were and that it was part of their duty to educate other people about the Mormon faith. He asked me if anyone else were in the house. I shook my head no, and he held out what I assumed to be a bible. Then he said that it was the Book of Mormon which had been given to his people by John Smith many years ago. He continued talking, and I really wasn't listening, but I leaned in as much as was physically possible without tipping over. Suddenly, he got up, stepped closer and sat on the arm of the love seat so that I could get a better look at what he was talking about; his thigh actually brushing against my shoulder. All religious thoughts ran screaming out of my head, chased by my sinful, horny nature. The short guy kept talking and, opening the Book of Mormon, pointing to various passages. The other guy looked a little uncomfortable; he just fidgeted with some pamphlets he had in his hand, but he would add a comment every so often, just enough for him to seem sociable. Even though short guy was deep in a one way discussion, he managed to keep his thigh on my shoulder. I pulled away slightly at first, out of nervousness, and he would immediately move his leg over to keep the slight pressure on me. I looked at his leg and back over my shoulder at his face and then over at the other guy. The hair on my arms joined the testosterone in my body and stood up.

At first I thought it was only me. I had learned a few painful lessons about assuming that other people were as interested in me as I was in them. I did tend to project a lot. Which was why I didn't try to do anything with anyone. It might have been the Twentieth Century, but it was still Mississippi and this Southern boy wasn't stupid. I kept looking back at him, then over at the other guy then down at my hands. Abruptly, the short one stopped talking. The sudden silence was almost deafening, competing with sound of the blood pumping through my body. I looked back at Short Guy and couldn't look away. I stared and stared. Then he reached over and put his left hand on my left shoulder, rubbing slightly, and holding the bible in his right, like he was trying to show a passage to me. He looked at the tall guy who was chewing the inside of his lip and fumbling with those pamphlets. Then Tall Guy got up from the sofa and came over to sit on the love seat next to me, showing me a glossy, colorful pamphlet with his left hand while his right hand rested tentatively on my leg, just above the knee. Obvious, but not actually crossing any lines. Extreme masculinity could still be claimed if need be. Just a group of religious seekers here. Nothing unusual.

I leaned back against the back of the love seat. Short Guy got up, put his bible on the coffee table, nudged us over and sat next to me on the too small piece of furniture. A Mormon cookie shell surrounding a rich quasi-Christian center. With nuts. I looked at him as he sat down; he just kept coming, leaning in until his lips touched mine. I often wondered why he did that. What kind of vibes did I put out? It wasn't like with Dr. Dennis a few years later; I wasn't wearing a headband. It was more primal. Like calling to like. Somehow, they knew. But the analysis of the situation came much, much later. At that moment, all I could think was "lips pretty, man pretty, smell nice." Yeah, two syllables was about my limit. God, his lips were very soft, just a little chapped, but still so soft. He stuck the tip of his tongue just inside my top lip. Then he pulled back and looked over at Tall Guy. I turned my head to him, and he kissed me. I was more ready this time which was good because his tongue went right past my lips and full on down my throat. Then he stopped, pulled back, and looked back at Short Guy. So I turned my head again.

Short Guy put his forehead against mine, turning his head back and forth, and said a little hoarsely, "Is there some place that's a little more private?" It's possible I might have actually gotten up from the love seat before he finished the question, leading the way to my bedroom which was just down the hall from the living room at the front of the house. The heavy drapes were pulled closed, and I didn't turn on the lights so we stood there next to my unmade bed, a human triangle. Short Guy started rubbing my chest while looking up at his friend who returned his stare with his hand on the small of my back, moving it slightly. I didn't know what to do. Theoretically, having sex with more than one person at one time is very exciting; in practice, however, it's a little confusing, especially when it is one's first sexual experience with an actual other person. I don't count the other experience as in any way sexual. I chose to do the first thing that came to mind, awkwardly rubbing Tall Guy's stomach and Short Guy's back which took thought and effort, a little like rubbing circles on your stomach while trying to pat your head at the same time. Actually, it was exactly like doing that; if I concentrated too long on one, I'd lose focus on the other, so I'd try to catch up. I'm nothing if not completely democratic.

Short Guy suddenly put his hand under my shirt and started rubbing. That was when the clothing became optional. As I was dressed in very little and the little I was dressed in could be taken off in about two complete movements, I won. Short Guy was just a little behind me, with Tall Guy being a bit more methodical. He took off his shoes, and his tie and white shirt. Then he took off his pants. He and Short Guy were wearing interesting underclothes and, being the enterprising young man I was, I decided to sexily help him take them off. As soon as I touched his undershirt, he pulled back and said politely, "I will take off my temple garments myself, thank you." So I just stood there, naked; sometimes it really pays to be first. After they had finished, we stood there, looking at each other. I looked at them a lot; they were turned mostly to each other.

Short Guy grabbed his pretty nice erection and asked, "You have any lotion?"

"Unh hunh," I said, nodding like a fool and hurrying to the bathroom right next to my bedroom. No lotion. I didn't want to go to my mother or my sisters' bedrooms as that would entail moving in front of quite a few windows. Then I looked over the bar separating the living room and kitchen. I ran through and grabbed the can of cooking spray sitting on the counter next to the stove. I walked back to my bedroom; they were standing face to face, slowly masturbating. But not touching. One of those moments where two people are in a bubble, away from the world. I shook the can to get their attention and removed the plastic top. "This is all I have," I mumbled, and I sprayed Tall Guy's dick before he could pull away. Then I sprayed Small Guy's penis, base to tip. Then me. Then I sprayed each again, just to be sure. I love all-purpose sprays. And it lubricated all right. It was an interesting, not at all unpleasant, sensation.

We each masturbated for a bit; then Short Guy started jerking me. Tall Guy rubbed my balls and then my legs and then my nipples. I again tried to be democratic, but that seemed to take a lot of concentration, and I just didn't have the mental capacity for it. Finally I surrendered and just stood there while they worked me over with one hand each and took care of themselves with the other. All the while their eyes were focused on each other. This went on for a timeless interval, and I think everyone was having a good time when we heard a car door slam. Someone had parked on the street in front of the house. I thought my heart would explode. We stopped our mutual satisfaction arrangement and listened. I've never listened harder in my life. Footsteps. Coming up the driveway. Oh god. Oh my god.

I found and pulled on my jogging pants while the guys were getting back into their temple garments. One leg bunched, and I had to pull it out before I could get it completely on. I got my t-shirt on (inside out – but I didn't notice that until later) while they were putting on their shirts and ties. And the doorbell rang. Tall Guy got his trousers on and his shoes; I helped Short Guy with his shoes after he'd pulled up his pants. I know we did all of this quickly, but it seemed to take forever. I got to the living room first and looked out the windows in the front door. There was to my grandfather standing outside the door, looking out at the yard, not through the windows in the front door. I saw his work truck parked on the road, its usual location when he visited during work hours because it leaked oil and he didn't want to mess up our driveway. Maybe, just maybe, he hadn't seen us come in the living room. I took a deep breath and held it. I looked back at the guys. Tall Guy had two buttons undone in the middle of his shirt, and they both were struggling a bit to get their ties back on and in place. Short Guy looked like he'd slept in his clothes. Grandpa turned around and saw me as I turned back around. I smiled and tried to open the door. My hand slipped on the knob. I had to use my shirt. I got the door opened and opened it wide. The guys had everything in place by then.

"Hey, Grandpa," I said, partially to let them know who this large man at my door was and partially to try to get back to some kind of normality, skewed though it might be.

He looked at me and at the men behind me; opened the screen door and came in and said, "Your Mamma wanted me to check on you."

"I'm fine. I'm feeling much better, thanks," I said as Grandpa looked at them. I continued in a loud rush, "These are some Mormons who came by to tell me about John Smith and Latter-day Saints."

"Joseph Smith," the tall one corrected, then he continued as he opened the screen door and held it as short one went through, "We have to be going." He stopped just outside and seemed to struggle for words, then said awkwardly, "Thank you for your help," and he joined his friend outside and walked away, ending my g-rated porn experience and leaving nothing but a Book of Mormon, four pamphlets, and (I later learned) a sock. I watched them walk down the road and turned back to my grandfather, forcing a smile.

Grandpa said, as if he couldn't think of anything else, "As long as you're okay, I better get back to work" and left, leaving me to inhale the buttery scent still lingering in the air.

The next afternoon after school, I got home and was working on homework in my room when I heard the phone ring. Mamma answered it, came to my room and said, "That was Grandpa. He wants you to come over and help him with something."

"What?" I asked.

"He didn't say."

I walked the two blocks, climbed the stairs to their porch, knocked and went in; Grandma and Grandpa were sitting in their living room.

"Sit down" Grandpa said, "we'd like to talk to you."

Oh great, I thought, they know.

Grandma said, accusingly, "Are you a Mormon?"

"Hunh?" I asked, feeling my heart start guilt-pumping faster, the way it always did when I'd been caught, or thought I'd been caught doing, something not quite heterosexual.

"Were those boys trying to convert you?" Grandpa said.

"No," I said, stretching the word out to a thoughtful three syllables. Not really understanding the question and not wanting to get into this. But also knowing that I was a big old convert. Or is it conversion when you never really were anything else? Never again would I claim to be straight-but-experimenting or bisexual. My orientation had crystallized. Right here in my grandparents' earth toned living room. This was the speed and unhelpful manner in which I was thinking. I needed to focus. Damn. My mind was usually my best part.

"Your Grandfather said that ya'll were in deep conversation and that you looked a bit upset. I'm telling you I won't stand for you becomin a Mormon. That's just like them Catholics," Grandma said, not caring that she made no sense.

"I'm not going to be a Mormon," I said, relieved that this was the direction the conversation was going. This I could handle. Then I added after I remembered, "Or a Catholic."

"They's nothing worse than going down the wrong path. And those boys might a been leading you to Hell."

"I think they were pretty good guys," I said. "They weren't leading me anywhere. It's not what you think. I promise."

"It looked deep," Grandpa said.

"If you become a Mormon, I'll never forgive you. You always did think too much," Grandma said.

"I'm not going to become a Mormon," I repeated, louder.

"And I'll be damned if I help you with anything ever again," she said, not listening and not letting go. God, that woman was a pit bull sometimes.

"It's your immortal soul we're worried about," Grandpa said, maybe trying to be placating. "We want the family together in heaven."

"I promise it's not what you think," I repeated to no one since no one was listening. Then I tried, "We were.." and I couldn't continue.

"Cause if you are a Mormon," he interrupted, not listening, "you'll never come into this house again."

"Not while we're alive," Grandma confirmed. "You might as well head on out to Utah and get yourself about ten or twelve wives if that perversion makes you happy."

"I'm not a Mormon!" I said, raising my voice, completely exasperated and wanting it to be over. So I said, "I'm just gay!"

"What?" Grandma said. Grandpa just sat there.

"I'm gay," I said, looking down at my shoes. I took a deep breath and continued, "We weren't talking religion when you came in, Grandpa; we were having sex. Or trying to." The last was almost mumbled. I took another deep breath, looked up at them and held it.

Grandma's usually olive complexion had gone pasty. Grandpa cleared his throat, tried to speak, but nothing came out. He cleared his throat again, and then said, "Well, that's bad too."

The doctors finally finished their tests and pronounced Grandpa if not fit then at least able to go home. The nurse helped me get him back in my car, and I went by the pharmacy to get his new prescriptions. Then I took him home, to the house I had once vowed never to enter again. The house I'd once been forbidden from entering.

"I appreciate you taking me to the hospital," he said, as I turned down his street.

"I'm glad I could."

He was quiet for a moment and then he said, "I want you to know something. Your grandmother and I are leaving you our house."

"What?" I said without thinking and then, "Why?" as I turned into his driveway and pulled the car into the carport and close to the back door.

"Cause it's the right thing to do. Kind of making amends."

"Grandpa, don't think you have to do that."

"Yes, we do," he said forcefully, "You're a good man, and I know in my heart that one day we'll all be together in glory. But I also wanted to make it right in this world." He looked at me, eyes bright, "I told a good man, my blood, that he couldn't come in my house. What kind of creature does that make me?"

"I guess I should be making amends too."

He nodded his head a little and said, "You already have. More than you know."

39

Brother God is gone!! Who would have thought it possible? Actually to be perfectly honest, I'm surprised that he lasted as long as he did. He just started getting more and more peculiar until there was no recognizing him.

First, every time he came to my class he kept asking me if he could talk to the whole class and ask them to join in his lawsuit. I kept putting him off, but the last two weeks he got pretty incensed; he kept handing me more papers to keep for him. Then, he would ask me if I read them and did I see why his lawsuit was so important, all while I kept directing him to my friend in Special Populations and telling her that I thought he was getting worse. And of course the school was on the ball and worked diligently to protect everyone (Security told him to stop doing whatever it was he was doing that was making me nervous). And he kept telling me that the government couldn't do "nothing to him because he knew where the bodies were hidden." Second, he went to the school's Learning Lab and proceeded to make an ass of himself. He walked in and went up to one of the tutors who was a very shy sheltered, home schooled child and said, "I need to send my resume to Disney Records Webb." No one, especially shy Tutor Child, knew what he meant; he meant he wanted to contact the Guinness Book of World Records and talk to them about his being heard on the radio – and whether or not it was a world record. The tutor put him on a computer so he could access Disney World's website. He took out a radio and started playing it very loudly which is against lab policy and asking everyone if they could hear his voice under the music. Anyway, my boss heard him from behind her cubicle wall and, because I had given her the heads up ("Trust me; he's crazy"), she rescued said tutor from a chaotic situation that had started to draw everyone's attention. It was at this point that my boss noticed that he had been drinking because he reeked of alcohol. I am of the opinion that crazy people shouldn't do anything to alter their personalities. Drinking can either turn someone's personality around one hundred and eighty degrees or magnify what's already there. Well, Brother God wasn't acting sane, so you can guess which way his personality went. He tried to get online and do his homework. My boss tried to help him, but she didn't have his password to access the computer. She kept asking him what his password was, and he just said, "Ask the President of these United States!" She finally said, "The President doesn't know either." He got exasperated and left, and my boss immediately called the Dean.

Brother God did eventually contact the Guinness Book of World Records. He showed me the letter in which they declined "at the present time" to look into his alleged record of being heard on the radio or television or computer; in fact, this was one of the "court documents" that I was to hold for him.

None of this was what got him kicked out of college and remanded to a psychiatric facility. He had been threatening the President for a while, and I had been complaining to the administration and relaying said threats. Then he decided to email the president directly to threaten him, as well as one of our deans, and the president of our little college. Events progressed amazingly fast after that. The threatened dean said that the FBI would be on campus to interview all of Brother God's teachers at 2 p.m. Friday afternoon. I usually leave at noon on Fridays; one of my educational perks is being able to finish with my office hours early in the week, so I can begin the weekend sooner. This campus is dead on Friday afternoons. I used to teach a late afternoon class on Fridays, and I could have gotten away with murder if I just timed it for Friday at about 2:30 p.m. So I was bored waiting for the appointment and standing outside my office when I saw Dr Ryan coming down the hall followed by some other man.

"Ya'll look real happy," I said, grasping for conversation topics because he'd seen me and they were heading my way so I couldn't duck back in my office and hide. Dr. Ryan intimidated me; I don't think he liked me. I was just tolerated, and that really bugged me.

"I'm just high on life," he said, maybe trying for a joke?

"And here I've been using crack all these years," I said. To absolute silence. "Kidding," I said, attempting a smile.

"Garland," he said, completely ignoring, or hopefully forgetting, the earlier interchange, "this is Dr. Crowley. He'll be presenting a lecture on poetry this afternoon."

"How do you do?" I shook his hand.

"Will you be at the lecture?" Dr. Crowley asked.

"Yes, he'll be there," Dr. Ryan answered, eyeing me rather pointedly.

"I can't," I said, "I'm meeting with the FBI." More silence.

"I swear I never know when you are joking," he said.

The lady from the FBI arrived promptly at 2 p.m. and met with all of Brother God's instructors in a large conference room.

"I've never met anyone from the FBI," I said excitedly, shaking her hand.

"How do you know?" she asked, and I liked her immediately.

Each of us told of our experiences, but I had the distinction of being the first to peg Brother God in the crazy hole. She was very frank and matter of fact about everything. She even commented on how he had "bonded" with me. In fact, there was certain information that I was the only one privy to. Like Brother God's political ambitions. He had said he was trying to be elected mayor of Rose Hill, Mississippi, but there were "secret forces" preventing him. "They" didn't want him to have any power whatsoever but he knew the people would see through this and elect him even though he wasn't technically on the ballot.

He shared all of this with me because I had mentioned in class one day that my grandmother was from Rose Hill, and Brother God thought we might be related. Judging by the other members of my family, we probably were. He wanted me to use my "political connections" to help him. I told him I couldn't use my political connections to help myself.

The government didn't want to put him in jail. They wanted him to get help. "It's really a shame," the FBI agent said, "if we had caught this ten or fifteen years ago, he'd probably be a functioning, valuable member of society." I gave her the "court documents" that I hadn't thrown away yet, and he was put in a mental facility in Georgia.

<h1 style="text-align:center">40</h1>

Caleb got grounded even more. He left to spend the night at his friend Nathan's house on Friday night, which is something he's done before; before he left, I called Nathan's grandfather (Nathan lives with his grandparents – another modern family), and asked if it was alright and said that I'd pick Caleb up at about 2 p.m. Saturday afternoon. The next afternoon, I called to say that I was on my way to pick him up, and Nathan's grandmother said, "He's not here."

"Where is he?" I asked, calmly, I thought.

"Oh, I took him and Nathan to meet one of Nathan's friends."

"Where does this friend live?"

"I didn't take them all the way to her house, it's in North Meridian, and I didn't have the gas; I just dropped them off at that burger joint. The friend's mom was gonna pick them up."

"Do you have their telephone number?" I asked the *extraordinarily* intelligent woman I was talking to.

"No, I prolly should a got one."

My heart started pounding faster and faster, and I could feel my face turning red. I called every hour on the hour basically asking, "Look lady, where's my kid?" Finally she said that Nathan had called and that she was going to get them and that she would drop Caleb off at home. Which she did. Caleb saunters into the house at 7:30 p.m. I was on the verge of being apoplectic and was actually seeing purple splotches in front of my eyes.

Caleb said, "I didn't think you'd mind since I was with Nathan," and I had to tell him that he would never be at Nathan's again since Nathan's grandparents obviously were too busy or too stupid to watch them. For me it was quite simple; he should have called and asked if he could go. He didn't see it that way. To him, I was Dr. Evil - Spoiler of Good Times, Grounder of the Innocent. He already couldn't use the television or his games; now he couldn't go anywhere either.

Then he showed me two discipline forms he had received from school last week; one was for getting an attitude with the principal, and the other was for calling his English teacher a "fat lard." He saved those until Saturday night because he knew that he wouldn't have been able to go anywhere Friday night if I had seen them first (I had to admit he did have some smarts), but that got him grounded for yet another week. And I put the video game in my car because Caleb told me that he "would just play it" while I wasn't home, which showed that he also had one of his mother's stupidest qualities-the absolute need to have the last word.

Sunday, I was relaxing on my favorite (and only) sofa in front of the television doing my favorite (and only) activity, channel surfing. It was just the sort of mindless activity that I loved after a long week's work with students who were masquerading as humans but were really vampires who delight in draining anything they could out of you and then flinging your lifeless carcass to the wayside; I wasn't in the best of moods. Caleb came in and sat next to me. He didn't say anything while I quickly looked through five or six hundred of my favorite channels, but I knew that he had something on his mind because this is just how he acts right before he tells me something like he's failing math or he thinks he broke the window in my car or it's really neat when something explodes in the microwave or he wants to go live with his dad in prison because I grounded him.

When he finally decided to speak, he said, "Can I ask you something?" He then raised his hand and put a little space between his thumb and index finger (about an inch) and said, "My penis is only this big!"

I can't say that I was expecting this, and I really didn't believe there was an adequate response, so I said hesitantly, "Uh huh?"

He said (again with his index finger and thumb), "It's only this big! Do you think it'll grow any more?"

I was not going to survive Caleb hitting puberty.

This was one of those circumstances which demonstrated a definite difference in attitude between my mother and me. My mother was wonderful in a crisis; if one of the kids accidentally cut off an arm, my mother would calmly pick it up, put it in a large zip-lock bag, conveniently stash it in her purse, put a rubber band on the wound to staunch the bleeding, grab the car keys, and get the kid to the hospital without losing any of her faculties. I, on the other hand, would fall apart or get sick or get so confused that I couldn't remember my name or the name of the kid that was hurt.

Talking about sex in very general terms didn't bother me; specifics, however, gave me the willies, pun intended. To give her credit, my mother was generally pretty laid back about sex, at least the female issues of sex. This despite having had to learn procreation from my grandmother, the Baptist minister's wife. Grandma had my mother firmly convinced that she would get pregnant from just sitting down after a man; everyone knows this only happens if one sits down too quickly. She didn't tell my mother anything when, at sixteen, Mamma married a man who was twenty-four. I can't think of anything crueler.

To help you understand my grandmother, when I was 18, she and I were talking and I said something about our dog being pregnant and my grandmother looked at me with this expression of horror and said, "Where did you learn that word?" So I know it couldn't have been easy.

But you'd think that in this age of basic cable that Mamma would be more okay talking about guy stuff. Wrong. She was okay with Trisha and Megan when they developed breasts and hips and periods. But she was not as good with guys. Which caused her to send Caleb in to talk to me when he first asked her about his penis size. I think it was really a continuation of a problem that I had noticed for a few years now; namely that my mother hadn't had sex in about twenty years and it was starting to tell; we were arguing about something or other – I forget what - and I think I might have offered to hire someone for her which I thought was the polite thing to do and would help improve her overall health and outlook.

Her response when I suggested an escort ,or even a male student in need of extra credit, went something like "You've got to be kidding;

I went through two horrible marriages and finally got rid of those fucking creeps. What makes you think I want anyone else even for a few minutes of fun?" – which just proved in my mind that she'd never done it right.

Back to Caleb. He now took the index fingers of both hands and enlarged them to porn star respectable size and said, "Some of the guys have penises this big."

And I just had to say, "Caleb, they're just eleven or twelve years old. There's no way. If it was that big, they'd trip all over themselves not to mention faint from blood loss when they did reach puberty and the appendage got excited. Are you sure they're that big? They might just be telling you that." My next question was: "Where have you seen all of these alleged large penises?"

He told me that he'd seen them in the restroom at school, and it had really only been two other boys; then he backed down a little and said, "Maybe they were just a little bit bigger." then he continued plaintively, "Do you think mine'll ever be big enough?"

I thought about it, and I wanted to say, "Probably not." Then I looked at him and said, "Caleb, soon you'll get taller and I'm sure your penis will get larger along with everything else; you'll be fine. I promise."

He said, "Is that what happened to you?"

I just said, "Sure."

He then said that the boys at school were talking about a pill that you could take to make it bigger, and that was what Nathan took and his was very big now. I told him that those pills were only good for taking your money, and if you took it, how could you guarantee that it was your penis that grew and not your left ear lobe (or Special Kay's unicorn horn)? He seemed to accept that okay. The next few years should be very interesting. I knew he would hit puberty soon; he kept coming over to me and telling me that he was growing a moustache – but I couldn't see anything – and that he was growing hair "everywhere but his privates." Everyone in the house was just a little leery when Caleb would say, "Hey, look at this."

I didn't think Mamma was going to enjoy these next few years too much. Last month she thought he was masturbating because she found all of these white spots on his dark blue sheets. I pointed out that if he did it that much the boy wouldn't be able to walk. It was her washing detergent that had caused the spots. Then she asked me what I'd say when we finally discovered that he was "doing the deed"

I said, "What do you think I'll say? I'll tell him to be careful." Too bad he didn't have a period to "regulate."

I wondered again about his thought processes when Caleb later told me that "masturbation was gay."

"What?" I asked, "How is masturbation gay?"

"Well, you're touching a man, aren't you?" he said.

"Technically yes, but it's yourself," I replied, logically.

"But it's still a man. That's so gay. If you touch yourself that way, you'll touch another guy that way," he countered, just as logically.

We'll just wait 'til the hormones really hit and see what he says then.

41

This sums up modern teaching in a nutshell: I came to work on Monday. After my first two classes, I went to my office where a student was waiting for me. She said, "Hey, Mr. Stewart! I just checked my grade, and I have an F in your class. Why?"

"Because you didn't take the first test," I said. Now I knew that she had been sick, but she had never come by to see what she had missed and what she needed to turn in.

So she turned her pouty lips in my direction, as well as straightening her back to make her boobs stick out a bit more, and said, "Can I make it up?"

"Yes, you can take a make up," I said, not looking at her breasts, knowing I shouldn't allow it but not wanting her to fail my class.

"Now?" she asked, pouting again since that worked well the first time.

"Okay." I got the test out for her even though she was three weeks late taking it and gave it to her. "I have to go to class," I said, "when you finish, just slide the test paper under my door." I left her in a lab near my office and went to my class. When I came back, there was the test on the floor of my office.. I picked it up and glanced at it. At the bottom of the page was written:

"Thank you so much for letting me make up this test.
You are the best teacher ever!
Thanks again Mr. Barnes."

Who needs gifts when I have the love of my (or Mr. Barnes'- whoever that is-) students? It was so much better in Saudi Arabia where students were placed under house arrest for not doing homework or taking tests. Of course, they were also beaten for making below a C. At least, I think they were; it was really getting difficult to remember that time in my life.

42

Spring Break just wasn't what it used to be. I didn't think that anyone who had kids (much less six of them — I was including my mother as she had really been getting on my nerves) would ever look forward to the quality time that you were forced to spend with said children. I knew it wouldn't be a good Spring Break when I got a phone call on Friday (the last day of class before the holiday) at 3 a.m. from my sister. She was in jail and wanted me to come and bail her out. It would appear that she had been arrested for driving under the influence and driving without a license. Since she doesn't have a car, I asked how she could have been arrested for driving. According to Lynn, she and Chris, her boyfriend (who had 3 teeth in his head, looked like he had been left in the sun too long, couldn't make - and didn't realize he couldn't make- a complete sentence — and I think was a dealer of sorts), had to go across town to this other man's trailer for "an urgent meeting." They were there for a while when another man (customer) came by and wanted Lynn to "run somewhere with him." Because he was unable to drive (whether this was from earlier partying or something that occurred at this particular trailer was not clear), my sister, being the altruistic and completely unselfish person that she is, magnanimously agreed to drive him. They were (according to her) no more than a mile or two from the trailer when the other guy passed out, and she couldn't wake him up enough for him to tell her where she was driving to, so she took a couple of left turns; that was when the cops pulled them over. She quickly pulled the keys out of the ignition and threw them out the window because someone had told her that you couldn't be arrested if the keys weren't in the car. The officers thought she threw drugs out the window and made her crawl around in the ditch until she found the car keys; I think the other guy was still passed out.

The police then administered a sobriety test and asked, "Have you been drinking, ma'am?"

"Hell, no! I ain't been drinking! That ass end of a turd has!" she said pointing to the passed out guy in the passenger's seat. "But I'm fine!" - Lynn tends to get a little loud and feisty when she's been drinking. She said she tried to explain that the other guy was too drunk to drive, and she had been just doing her Christian duty when they arrested her. Then she told them that her grandfather was a Baptist minister and that I was a college professor and that we wouldn't sit by while she was thrown in jail.

I told her that I would not bail her out and that I would appreciate it if she wouldn't use my name, ever. Not only didn't I have the hundred and eighty-six dollars necessary, but I had sworn when I bailed her out for her first DUI, and she had promised faithfully that she'd pay me back –she didn't- and that it wouldn't happen again. This was a year after her first stint in rehab and the reason that she went for a second time.

She called us to say she "didn't know why they had put her in with all these drug addicts; her only problem was drinking." I asked her if she remembered that time when she smoked crack every day for four years. She said she didn't know what I was talking about. Then I told her to ask her therapists what the clinical definition of insanity is. I swore she would never guilt me into helping her again. She then called back and wanted me to call a bail bondsman for her.

I did, but as soon as I told the guy who it was that wanted to be bailed out, he said, "That girl ain't worked in fifteen years. I won't do it unless you sign for it." So for the next three days, Lynn called collect at least five times a day at about $3.50 per call and begged, pleaded, demanded, threatened, then cried. I accepted the charges on a few calls until I couldn't take it anymore and stopped taking the calls completely. There was nothing I could do. There was nothing I wanted to do. I was sure I was doing the right thing. But it was one of the hardest things I've ever had to do.

Of course this would be the weekend that my mother had to take Megan to cheerleading competition in Biloxi which is the actual reason that I didn't have money. We had had to come up with about five hundred dollars for the trip – hotel, food, fees. I had wanted to go and take the other kids, but we couldn't afford the entry fees for all of us, or the gas for the two hundred mile trip. Megan said she understood, but I don't think she did.

That meant that I was by myself. I tried to intercept all of Lynn's calls, but I couldn't get them all, and the kids figured out where she was almost immediately because it said "Lauderdale Correctional Facility" on the caller I.D. when she called. Trisha and Megan couldn't have cared less. Allie, Caleb, and Diane did care and accused me of being a horrible person because I wouldn't even let them talk to their mother who was in jail, and they went through the house trying to find spare change to help pay to get her out.

The icing on the cake was finding out that Allie's father (Joey) and Caleb's father (Byron) were also incarcerated in the same facility. Joey was in for public drunk and indecent exposure – he was wearing a skimpy pair of blue jean shorts and nothing else; his "business" was hanging out all over the place. Byron was in jail for agreeing to put roofs on people's houses, taking part of the money from them, and then never returning – this was about the fourth or fifth time he'd been arrested for this. Lynn passed notes to them and later told the kids that they should write their dads so they [the dads] wouldn't feel so lonely – I won't reprint what I had to say about that.

Lynn finally got in touch with Chris, who finally realized she wasn't coming back to the trailer after three days; he bailed her out on Sunday afternoon, which coincidentally was the same day that my mother and Megan got back home; Megan's cheerleading squad came in second place which meant they would be going to nationals- which would be even more expensive. I will not even begin to tell you how I ranted and raved. Not only about Lynn, but also about the kids who every three seconds would turn to me accusingly and say, "There's nothing to do in this house, and you kept our mother in jail."

To make matters worse, I had done something to my left shoulder and, as I'm not known for enduring pain silently, I yelled, I screamed, I hollered. When my prescription queen mother got back, she saw my (and the kids') frazzled dispositions and asked me if I would like a muscle relaxer. I said, "What the hell" and took that as well as the pain pill that she thrust at me. I woke up Tuesday afternoon with a head full of cotton, a bladder full of pee, a stomach full of nothing, and a shoulder that still hurt; my mother just looked at me with an impish grin and said, "If you hadn't got up by tomorrow, I was going to call someone."

Wednesday afternoon, I found myself going to get pizza. I know I never have any money and feeding all of us at a restaurant took the per capita income of Uruguay, but I was basically guilted into it by two occurrences, both of which were overheard conversations. The first was Allie talking to one of her friends and telling this girl that "all we ever eat around here is tuna fish and hotdogs." This made me feel bad enough, but then I heard my mother talking to one of her friends on the phone and saying that she had eaten so much Macaroni and Cheese that "she had to board up her ass at night to keep the rats out." Five pizzas should be enough.

43

Thursday should have been a great day. It started out okay enough. Megan was staying with her friend Kailea; Allie was staying with her friend Amanda. Trisha had been in her room and hadn't been seen in days; I just kept sending in food and asking her if she had leprosy. Caleb and Diane played cards and watched T.V. without beating each other to bloody pulps, and my mother sat on the sofa reading. Then we got a phone call from a second cousin of mine saying that my father's sister (Aunt Gayleen) was dying. I was really heart broken. As was my mother who had been within twenty miles of her just last weekend when she and Megan had been in Biloxi (my aunt lived in Gautier –just a little further down Interstate 10). The most we could get out of my cousin was that my aunt had cancer and wasn't expected to live more than another week and that she had asked about us.

I hadn't seen Gayleen (I've never called her "aunt") in over six years. She had never seemed to change; I remember an older, short, overweight, mannish woman who dearly loved to sing-and anything to do with singing. I wish I had had a good reason for not seeing her. I didn't. She and I always seemed to relate well to each other, but only when we happened to be near one another, and neither of us went out of our way to meet. I say this as if I think it was mutual. It was more my doing. My father died when I was two. We moved up here when I was four. I would visit Gautier a couple of weeks during the summer when that grandmother was alive, but that dwindled away after she died and I grew up. I never really had anything in common with those people except a last name. All of my cousins were construction workers who barely finished high school or didn't finish and just got their G.E.D's. I had nothing against construction workers, but I really didn't have anything for them either. But Gayleen, because I was the only child of her favorite brother, had tried to include me.

So Friday morning, my mother and I got up at 5 a.m. and drove two and a half hours to the coast to see her for what most likely would be the last time. We made record time and didn't kill each other during our enforced "together time" although Mamma just couldn't keep quiet about my driving ("You think you're close enough to the yellow lines? We're gonna go off the road!!"). We got to Gautier and turned down a road that used to be wilderness but, with the influx of casinos, had since become full of subdivisions. Off of the main road was another road (Stewart's Bluff Road) that was still heavily forested. It had only been paved these last ten years, but it still brought memories of too much dust on hot afternoons and too many mosquitoes just before dusk.

At the end of the road on the bluff of a lake fed by the Singing River was my Aunt Betsy's house. Gayleen lived with her; she had since my grandmother, whose house was once next door but has since been demolished by time and neglect, had died. She had never lived on her own. And she never married. And she spent more than a few years in Whitfield, the State Asylum, because she didn't take my father's death well; when she returned, she had needed a guardian. She never talked a lot about her experience there except to say that she had had to sit next to an ex-judge who kept hitting the table with his shoe and yelling, "Case dismissed!" and saying for as long as I can remember, "I better not do that or they'll send me back to the loony bin and I'll get them electric shocks again." I really think she got electric shocks. What an incentive to stay, or pretend to stay, sane. Gayleen always did hear different music and her greatest joys in life were cigarettes, root beer, fussing, and, of course, singing.

We got to the house, got out of the car, and went in. My Aunt Betsy just looked at me and said, "The nurse just put her to bed. Go on back." I went down the hall and walked in to her room. I wouldn't have recognized her if I hadn't known it was her. She'd lost so much weight; her face was so sharp. She was in a hospital bed that was angled slightly (head down; feet up). She took one look at me and said, "There's that handsome man!" I knelt down on the floor, and we made small talk for a minute. Then she said, "I gotta get out of this damn bed" and got up, slowly and carefully. She held my hand and walked with me to the living room; she had a walking stick, but I noticed that it never touched the ground; she just seemed to carry it with her. She sat down in her favorite rocking chair and put an oxygen tube under her nose.

The four of us just communed for a while. My mother and Gayleen reminiscing about old times when the most they had to worry about was getting a Pepsi at the local gas station, way before my mother's widowhood or my aunt's electric shocks. Another lifetime when my mother had been her favorite sister-in-law; Gayleen hated all of the other wives of her other brothers. Gayleen, holding my mother's hand, told us she had a tumor in her stomach. And I could see that her stomach was very distended. She had lost both of her breasts many years ago in a radical mastectomy and, because she said that "no one was interested in her tits anyway," had never worried with them again and was actually thrilled not to have to wear a bra. Her feet were extremely swollen which was why her bed was angled; that condition had just started a few days before. I asked what the doctor had said. She didn't know.

"Why not?" I asked.

As soon as the doctor had told her that she was going to die, Gayleen had said, "What the hell good are you then?" and stormed out. Aunt Betsy had stayed to talk to him. The tumor was inoperable and was growing too rapidly, and she was too weak to withstand chemotherapy or radiation. Gayleen said, "And the worst thing is now I have to wear a diaper!" Then she said, "Come on the porch with me; I gotta have a cig."

I was just about to say "That's a stupid habit" (a common argument between us) when I realized how pointless that would be. We went on the porch and enjoyed a comfortable, companionable silence while she smoked and I watched the white clouds; she exhaled toward the ceiling, the smoke gradually fading into nothingness.

She then looked at me and said, "Hey, let's go get something to eat." I thought she meant get something from the kitchen so I followed her inside, but she started putting on her jacket and combing her hair.

Mamma said, "Do you think you should be going out?" but Gayleen just looked at her, and in no time she, my mother and I were comfortably ensconced in our minivan and on our way to Angel's Seafood Restaurant which was just down the road and had the best seafood around. We went inside, with Gayleen taking a little longer than usual due to her walking stick and her portable oxygen tank on a little rolly cart, and got a good table in the smoking section.

She looked up and saw her old boss from when she had worked in the cafeteria of the local community college. "There's Dean Anderson!" she said in a voice that carried all through the restaurant. "He's the man who fired me when I wouldn't let him screw me on the stainless steel table next to the slicer." Dean Anderson didn't stay long after that, and the woman with him didn't look too pleased either.

Gayleen talked and talked, and Mamma and I were real quiet and listened; it wasn't until much later that I realized that she hadn't really eaten anything. We got back to Betsy's house and, as we were walking back inside, my mother whispered to me that Gayleen would never go back to bed if we didn't leave.

So we took them inside and Mamma said, "Well, it's been great seeing ya'll but we better be going." I helped her back to her room and put her to bed. I angled the bed exactly as it was when I first got there, and I covered her up with the huge quilt she had on the bed.

She looked up at me, enormous bright eyes in that gaunt face and said, "You gonna come back for the funeral?"

We were way beyond pretending she wasn't going to die, so I said, "I didn't think you were much of a believer."

"I'm not, but what the Hell? I won't be there, and it'll make some people [she pointed to the other room and the other aunt] stop their yapping. You better come to the wake. These assholes have been pestering me to wear a dress, so I am. And I told them that since they had finally got me in a dress [this is true; she'd worn pants all the time I'd known her] they had better have the casket lid open all the way so people can admire my waiflike beauty."

I laughed and said, "Sure, I'll be there."

Then she looked up and said, "But I have talked things over with the funeral director, and we got an understanding."

"About what?"

"Nothing. Just be at the viewing." Then she settled back firmly on her pillow, "And you better be at the damn funeral too." She grabbed my arm, her eyes blazing, "You come and help sing me to Glory, you hear?"

"I'll be there, but I can't believe it's that important to you. You never even liked the church down here. Last time I went to church with you, you called the minister a 'god fearing little prick' and said you'd rather be in Hell any day of the week because only boring piss heads went to Heaven."

She smiled, shrugged and said, "Well, what you want me to say? Best to cover all my bases." She let her head drop back to the bed, closed her eyes and whispered, "I don't think I ever really belonged here. Mamma said I did, so did your daddy. But it watn't true. That place they sent me was the true Hell, and I'd a done anything not to go back." She opened her eyes and looked at me, "Your daddy woutn't a let them send me there." She sighed, "But he was gone by that time." She drew herself up, "Well, that's the past. And I can't stay there, even though I want to sometimes. With your daddy. And mine. And my Mamma." Her eyes glistened and seemed to focus on something out the window, "I hope they waiting for me." She looked back at me, "I lost any belief in god-on-earth I ever had in the looney bin. That watn't a place for god, and they just forgot me there. But I didn't lose my faith. And I didn't lose my humanity. I'm talking real humanity, not what these self-righteous pieces-of-shit call humanity; that's just something they can do so other people can see them doing it and call them good Christians. I always wanted more … something, faith maybe. But I learned not to say too much until I was older and knew they couldn't send me back. The only thing that kept me whole was the singing. They'd hook me up to that machine, and I let a loud chorus go in my head. Usually by the time the treatment was over, only one voice was left, my voice, echoing in my head. It watn't enough. And I miss that chorus. That's why you gotta come. Everybody together, singing and talking about how good I was, that could make God forget. And forgive me for these past forty years. Then he'll let me be with those I love." She stared at me for a minute longer and then said, "I guess I'll be seein ya."

Eight days later, we were back for the wake. Aunt Betsy had said on the phone that Gayleen died in her sleep, peacefully, with no pain. Mamma and I went straight to the funeral parlor. Mamma had to go to the bathroom, so I went into the main viewing room by myself. The first thing I saw was my Aunt Betsy, sitting there surrounded by well-wishers. She had this smile fixed on her face, but she almost looked angry. I waved to her but didn't feel like enduring everyone's sympathy, so I went to the casket. There Gayleen was in the most god awful hot pink full length evening gown I'd ever seen. It hurt my eyes to look at. God. Then I noticed that her right arm had been placed diagonally across her chest and someone had put a big yellow daffodil over the arm. In fact, it looked like some of the daffodils in a vase next to the coffin. I reached down and moved the flower just a little. Yep. The middle finger was positioned strategically. She was giving the bird I guess to the universe. Mamma walked up; I pointed to Gayleen's hand and smiled. Mamma said, "It looks like she found a way to piss the family off for most of eternity. I know Betsy will never forget it."

The next morning was the funeral. I think half of the town showed up. We sat through the usual glossed over version of a life that was in no way ordinary. Then everyone stood and sang "The Old Rugged Cross." It had been her favorite. I remember summer vacations, sitting on the screened in front porch at night overlooking the lake, praying for a breeze to break the heat and Gayleen singing that song in a quiet voice. I did not have a good voice, but I sang. Loud. She'd asked me to, and it was something I could do. Singing her to Glory. Everyone else sang as loud as they could too. I could feel the charge in the air. I closed my eyes; I swear I could feel the moment that her soul was catapulted over by the force of our singing to some place where she wouldn't suffer anymore.

After the last notes died away and everyone had sat back down, the minister went back to the podium. "The last time I spoke to Sister Gayleen, she said that the only thing she'd ever really wanted in life that she never got was a standing ovation." He stopped and I could see that tears were starting to fall down his face. When he spoke again, his voice cracked slightly, "Let's give our Sister her final wish." He started clapping; then, everyone started clapping and got to their feet. We continued clapping as the pall bearers carried her out.

44

This week had the coldest weather we had had for a while and it was Spring Fest where clubs and organizations show their spirit and try to make some money. It was just above freezing. The Multicultural Club was planning a dunking booth for Wednesday, and I'd gotten quite a few people to commit to it. The Wednesday before had been just perfect. Then the cold set in. And the rain.

But Wednesday dawned clear and just a bit crisp. A fellow teacher who had a truck (or her husband did) with a two inch gizmo on the back went to get the dunking booth, but it came with no instructions. I'm not in the least mechanically inclined, but with the help of a few people, we got it set up in the right position. Then I went over and asked a couple of the maintenance people who were helping set up other clubs' displays about water to fill it. They looked at me like I had just farted. Then they pointed all the way across from where we were and said that the hoses were over there and that we should have thought of that before we set everything up. I actually had asked the week before that we be placed near a hose – but sometimes I forget my place in the grand scheme of things. My co-advisor took the initiative, called the fire department, and within five minutes they were on campus filling the booth. It was great.

We had a great time, and we made a nice bit of money. I was about the third person in; I hurled insults at everyone and was dunked a few times. After I got out, I was dripping and talking to one of my students and I noticed that her eyes wandered away from mine. I looked and saw the next person in the dunking booth go under for the first time. My student sighed and said, "Seeing him in that wet t-shirt makes me feel like I'm at the beach by myself."

She obviously didn't know that I'd been exercising for weeks and weeks. I decided to go drip somewhere else.

When I got back to my office, I checked my voice mail while I was changing. I heard a quiet voice on the machine. It was my fraidy lady, the student I had mouthed encouraging words to even though they were kind of empty, a shell of fake caring because I was busy. A very small voice said, "Mr. Stewart, I won't be in class today. My son passed away. I have to make funeral arrangements. I'll call you to find out what I missed." I just sat there staring at the phone. This lady had in the midst of her grief thought to call and tell me she wouldn't be here. And it dawned on me how important school must be to her. And how important I was to her. The world really was good. Mostly. I had to remember that.

45

Megan wanted a cell phone. I hated phones of any kind, but particularly those that I had to carry with me. My mother got me a cell phone for my fortieth birthday and I accepted it, but only because it was hooked into her plan somehow, and I had maybe three thousand minutes a month that rollover. My calculations showed that I had approximately fifty-eight million that I had to use before the end of the year.

I was never one of these people who could talk on the phone for hours and hours endlessly cooing or chuckling; I said what I needed to say, then I hung up. The kids, however, did not take after me in this. The phone was constantly ringing, and it was never for me. Or my mother. Or Trisha since she got a boyfriend. Right now, the phone effectively belonged to Megan and Caleb with them acting as Regents over this private fiefdom called BellSouth. And they fought and fought over it. Throw in the internet, and it became even more special.

The kids here at this college were just as bad; I couldn't tell you how many times a person's cell phone has rung in my class, usually while I am giving the lecture of a lifetime – one that will go down in history and change the lives of anyone who happens to be listening, and the student will answer it without thinking that he or she's in class. Or I would be walking down the sidewalk between classrooms and on more than one occasion I've heard someone say into that little hunk of plastic, "Hey MarcQuavion, 's up?" Then I'd hear them say, "Nuttin', what you doing?" *ARGHH!!*

I threw in that name because one of my students told me that my name was too boring, and I asked her to come up with a jazzier name for me and that was what she came up with. It was either MarcQuavion or Ju'Shantyunna or Tekerriyatah. I told her that I thought she and her friends were playing a joke on me; I mean I could just see her and her friends sitting around elbowing each other in the ribs, laughing hysterically, and saying, "He thought I'd name my child Teriyaki".

I didn't know how many times I'd been reading my first day rolls and calling out names in class when I would come to a name, let's say Jaterrionna, and I would give it my most valiant phonetic effort, but I would still mangle it beyond anything that could be repaired.

After I tried a few times, the student would rescue me by saying, almost in a disgusted fashion, "My name is Jaterrionna – I was named after my mama, my daddy, and my uncle that lives down the street." I would then apologize and pronounce it exactly like they said. They would smile, digest that momentary victory, then say, "But everybody calls me Terry."

Some of the names were almost lyrical. And when it worked, the results were beautiful like Meissa or Heloniafai (pronounced "Hell – on – a –fa") or Kimmea. Then there were other hunter/gatherer wannabes like Skip or Chase or Scout or Hunter. Of course, no one is ever satisfied with a name, so the trend usually lasts only a generation or two. One of my students' names was, and I'm not making this up, Malayzha VaNekia Kwaterrionna Jones. She was a very nice young lady about twenty-five years old. And she was pregnant with a little girl. I asked her what she was planning on naming her daughter, and she said it was a toss up between Molly and Susan. My grandmother had friends named Louver Dee, Rubeena, Rooner Claudette, Lula Clotille and Ruby Mayzelle; the best name she ever told me was Forkson Fair.

I do get such a kick out of names; there was a student in my class a few years ago whose name was Arcula. I dutifully pronounced it exactly the way it was spelled, "Ar-coola," putting extra emphasis on the "oo" and the "la." A very attractive, well-dressed woman sitting in the front raised her hand and said, "It's pronounced Erica." I looked at the name on the roll, then up at her again and raised an eyebrow. She laughed and said, "Don't even ask."

Megan just had to talk to Biff or Reardon or Colt. These names just killed me; they weren't even good hunter/gatherer names. In fact, they sounded more like porn stars (Well, like the porn stars I liked to watch anyway). Before he died, Les used to say that everyone has a secret drag queen name; I think my grandmother might have actually said something like this too. No, what she said was that everyone had a name that made them "morally suspect." Who knows where she got that from? Whatever. Whether for drag or moral turpitude, take the name of your first pet and the name of the street you live on; mine is Prince Manning. This is really a lot of fun in class; it livened things up considerably. Some of the best names were Buffy Orso, Suki Blasst, Shakes Myster, and Binki Chapperelle. Then there was Muffy Arcadelphia or her cousin Kitty Arcadelphia both of which just make me giggle. The worst, in my opinion, were Midnight Bunting, Dinky Dogwood and Fudge King which I think might have been my grandmother's.

Megan had to talk to all of these people, so they can talk about what just happened at school which I might add ended two seconds ago. I took my cell phone and hid it, but first I looked to see that I still had 57.5 million minutes left; it's not the fact that I needed this many minutes, it's just that I wanted them; you never know when I might need to call Uzbekhistan or the Dalai Lama.

Then Megan looked at me and said with those big blue eyes, "When am I gonna have my own phone?" And I wanted to say, "When Hell freezes over," but I simply said she would get her own phone when we were able to comfortably fit back in the middle class without the need for pushing, shoving or lubricants. She said, "I don't understand you at all."

And the problem was that Biff, Boffo and Slade all had their own cell phones, with about as much to talk about as MarcQuavion, and phone lines into their bedrooms. I don't understand.

Megan and Caleb got into a few knock-down-drag-outs over the use of the phone. Since Caleb turned twelve ("preteen" as he likes to say), he has made it a fairly regular practice to give his phone number to any girl aged nine, ten, eleven, twelve, and (on one memorable occasion) sixteen; he favored the scattershot approach. And they called him. Constantly. At all hours. Often they didn't believe us when we told them that he was not here; they would hang up and call back five minutes later.

My mother and I were sitting on the couch the other night, and Caleb came in with a piece of paper. He handed it to me and said, "These are the only girls I'll talk to from now on; tell everyone else I'm not home." He was practicing for a position in upper management somewhere; I shan't repeat what I said.

And for the internet, Caleb wasn't allowed to use it because a few weeks ago I came home, and he had a CD in the computer and the volume up *really* loud. I didn't really know what the song was because the only word I heard was "Fuck." In fact, that seemed to be the only word that this guy was saying – to some really nice background music- and I wasn't prepared to be gracious about it unless Caleb could prove that the guy had Tourrette's Syndrome. Caleb said he'd burned the song and that everyone at school really liked it.

Amazingly, it's not just your kids you have to worry about. Last week I walked into the bedroom, and Caleb was on the phone. I knew he'd been on the phone for at least thirty minutes, and I was about to tell him to get off. Then I noticed he was saying things like "Yes, ma'am" and "No, ma'am." and "I don't know." I thought he was talking to his girlfriend. I asked him who he was talking to; he put the phone on his chest and said, "Amanda's mom." So I asked him why he was talking to that girl's mother and he said, "She wants to know why I broke up with Amanda." Amanda was ten.

I took the phone and asked, "This is Caleb's uncle. May I help you?"

"I just wanted to know why he thinks my little girl isn't good enough for him. He's broke her heart." I didn't know that extreme bitchiness could be transmitted so clearly, but it sure was. And for some reason, I could just see this woman with dirty blond hair, in a torn bathrobe with curlers in her hair, a cigarette and a beer in one hand while drawing out her next tattoo with the other. And at that moment, I knew that Amanda was not good enough for my Caleb. I didn't want him anywhere near that gene pool. I told Amanda's mom (I never found out her name) that not only did I not want Amanda to call back, but I also didn't want her to call back either; I think I might also have added that the kids were too young for her to be that involved in their lives and that it was obviously taking time away from her meeting the Hell's Angel of her dreams and planning her next pregnancy. She didn't call back.

46

It was almost time for finals, that wonderful time of the semester in which students will try to do in two weeks what they didn't do in sixteen. I just loved it. One student came by (one that I hadn't seen in three weeks and had been planning to put her picture on a milk carton) and asked if she had "missed anything." I smiled. Another student asked what he could do to pass my class; I said, "Take it again." He then asked if he could do anything for extra credit. I growled at him. This was the time of the semester when you didn't mess with the instructor; we'll cut you.

And then there were the "fraidy ladies"; these were non traditional students (about 50 years old although they could be either older or younger – they didn't even have to be female) and very nervous. I called this type of student a "fraidy lady" because the world has not been kind to them and they're returning to school to finally get back on a track that was derailed by unplanned pregnancy, marriage, general stupidity, or all of the above.

One lady came to us using the time-honored process that involved a very abusive marriage; she had absolutely no self-esteem. None. He had beaten it out of her. I had had students like this before, but this one was a definite challenge. She cried a lot. And I don't mean gentle, quiet tears falling; I mean full gale force sobbing that brings to mind a hungry child lost in the wilderness. To be honest, I (and her other teachers) had decided she was becoming a sympathy junky and that we needed to be selective in the sympathy we showed her. And at the end of the semester, I really didn't have a lot of sympathy to give. So this student came to class and sat quietly, but I noticed that she was holding her neck; she'd done that before as part of her sympathy package, or she'd held her arm and said that she "fell off of" her front porch ,but she wouldn't go to the doctor.

I continued the lecture. After about twenty minutes, I noticed that tears were falling, and she was trying to get up out of her desk. So I said, "What's wrong?" as matter-of-factly as I could. She continued to try to get up but was really having a problem. I went to try to help her, grabbed her hand, and she immediately fainted. I felt like fainting too until I realized that I needed to be in charge.

The other students were wonderful. We lowered her to the floor and moved the desks out of the way. The guy who sat behind her put a satchel under her head. I ran out of the class and asked the nice ladies in the Business Office, which was just across the hallway from my classroom, to call security. And then I waited. And waited.

When the security officer did show up, he looked at me, at the student lying obliviously on the floor, at the desks that were no longer in straight rows and said, "What's the problem?"

"Problem, what problem?" I wanted to say, but I bit my tongue. He finally helped me get her situated; she woke up and didn't remember anything. I insisted that she go to the doctor and one of the young ladies in the class agreed to take her. Then I cancelled the rest of class. I mean we had been sitting around panicking for a good fifteen minutes, and I just didn't have it in me to pick up the lost threads of my lecture. Plus, I didn't think it would have looked sympathetic at all if I had insisted that the students return to their seats and continue taking notes – notes that I could write on the board only after I stepped over the body in the floor. That would be a bit much. So I told the students to exit quietly, and if anyone asked them which class let out early, to say, "College Algebra." Best to cover all of one's bases.

47

My cousin BB called last night to tell me that he had purchased a bull and that since it "didn't look like I'd ever get married and have kids" he decided to name it after me. He said that he just loves going to the back door, opening it and seeing "Garland all over the other cows." He said that in no time there'd be "little four-legged Garlands all over the place," so I didn't have to worry about my lineage. I thanked him.

Trisha turned eighteen. It was a very low key affair; she took it the way she did most things – calmly. I didn't know where she got that. So I was looking forward to her turning eighteen with no major upheavals. Her birthday was May 5th. Cinco de Mayo. We used to watch the celebrations in Mexico on television when she was a little girl, and I'd tell her that they were celebrating her birthday. Trisha came in my bedroom and sat down next to me. Since she never does this, I assumed that I must be dying or some such. Trisha nonchalantly said, "I need to ask you a question, but I want you to know that you can say no." I just looked at her and kind of nodded my head. Then she said, "Can I spend the night at Kyle's place sometimes on the weekends?"

The world stopped and my mind went into overdrive. "Arghh!! How dare you!! Do you think we run a brothel here? Why can't you and Whose-its get your jollies on a dirt road like all the other kids? You're just eighteen; you don't know enough about life yet. Believe me, you might regret this later on. You think this guy is the one, but are you really sure? What if he isn't? What if he's just the one right now? I'm not saying he is or he isn't, but what if? This will forever change

177

your life, and you're just being too damned calm about it!" This is what I thought while my mind sputtered and choked.

And then I looked at her. She had gone about asking in exactly the right way. She wasn't making a big issue of it, and she left the door open for me to say no. Because she knew I wouldn't. I wanted to. Desperately. But I couldn't. Trisha must find her own way. I can only hope that I'd shown her how to make good decisions. She and Whatyamacallits had been dating for a year; they were good together. I didn't know if they would last, but I had to trust her judgment. She was a good kid. She was about to finish high school, had a part time job at a pharmacy; in fact, she said she wanted to be a pharmacist. Damn it! So I said, "Okay, just remember to be careful."

She kissed me on the cheek, said "Thank you" and left. Damn, Damn, Damn, Damn, Damn.

48

Caleb decided to attack me the minute I got home. He wanted to play soccer over the summer, and he signed up for tryouts unbeknownst to me or my mother. I told him, for the same reasons he couldn't play baseball, that I didn't think it was a good idea. Diane was playing softball; in fact, I was supposed to take her to a game at 6:30 p.m. if it wasn't called off because of rain, and it was just too much to have two playing sports. I was going to be teaching four nights a week this summer, so my mother would have to get Diane to her games two nights a week; there was no one else to do it. Plus there was the fact that I didn't have the money for anything else.

The end of the school year was horrible in supposedly-free public school. Caleb and Allie each needed $9 for their respective Spring Flings. Of course, it being public education; no one was actually forced to go. Those who couldn't pay the money would get to read in the library and watch the kids who did pay get on and off of the various rides. Diane needed six dollars for her Spring Fling (and a lunch), Megan needed $147.75 for cheerleading camp which was required for her to be a school cheerleader, and Trisha's annual cost fifty dollars. It was not even the tenth of the month, and I only had $8.53 to last until the thirty-first.

So Caleb basically told me that he was going to stay after school for tryouts anyway, and I threatened him to within an inch of his life.

I came home to Caleb yelling and Diane running around trying to get ready for the game. It was misting outside and, to be completely honest, I really wanted the game to be cancelled. God, I was tired.

Caleb and Allie decided to go with Diane and me. We got there, and Caleb and Allie immediately ran in opposite directions, so they could sit with their friends; I was just not cool enough. I took Diane to her coach, Ms. Dabner, who told me that the shirts would cost eighteen dollars and the visors, which she felt every child needed and had their numbers on them plus they were just so darned cute, would cost eight dollars. I asked what happened to the sixty-five dollars I'd already paid for Diane to be part of the soft ball team, and which I had been told would cover all of the costs, and the woman just looked at me; Diane told me later that I had humiliated her and that she could never look Ms. Dabner in the face again. So I dutifully made my way to my seat in the bleachers holding Caleb's bat and glove because he was supposed to be practicing in the batting cage, which was the original reason that he accompanied us; I also found myself holding Allie's purse which she had to have for her lip gloss, and Diane's bottle of water and jacket in case it rained. I sat on the back row and tried to get in a "soft ball" frame of mind.

A few seats in front of me was a guy (let's call him Mullet Man) and his 3-or-4 year old son (Little Mullet). Next to him was this extremely thin woman with very blonde hair and no front teeth. Oh, and I must mention her breasts. They were very large and didn't seem in any way to correspond to her overall size. I also gathered that they were new because she kept pointing them at everyone (Another woman – I'm assuming a friend - came by her and said that they hadn't seen her in a while and my my didn't she look different. Breast Woman just nodded her toothless head and said that she'd lost weight – yeah, in her left eyebrow). Across the row from me was an elderly couple in their late sixties with a forty year old looking woman sitting in front of the man who kept snapping her bra strap, so I'm going to assume they knew each other. The elderly woman ignored this by-play but at one point before the game actually started, she turned to me and said, "You know I have a golden retriever that I keep in the house." I just smiled and nodded my head. Then the game started. Diane was on the South Lauderdale II team, and they were playing Chunky. Diane's team was milling around third base waiting for the Chunky team to come out and greet each other before beginning. Then I saw the Chunky team. I didn't know there was a nuclear reactor in Chunky. Either that or some of those girls were abusing steroids. They were that big. And they had attitude. Diane's team of hobbits didn't stand a chance. The final score was 14 – 0. I thought at one point that the hobbits might stand a chance because the Chernobyl team couldn't pitch. I meant the pitcher (whose muscles were actually bulging) couldn't throw a straight pitch if her life depended on it. It went way up, it went way down, it went way over there. At the top of the second half, that girl was walking everyone. Or so it looked for a few minutes. Then we got a series of girls (Diane included) who decided to move the bat over to where the ball was thrown no matter where it was actually pitched. They all struck out pretty quickly.

There was a period of about fifteen minutes of the game that I missed because Allie came to me to say that Caleb had told her and her friend to "fuck off" and then called them "dickheads." Caleb claimed that Allie had hit him in the back with a stick and showed me (there was a red welt), but he didn't deny saying anything. So I dealt with that for a while and went back to my spot. Those parents were yelling all kinds of things at those girls: "You better hit that ball" and "Catch it! Catch it! What's wrong with you?" They took it way too seriously. Then I had to miss another few minutes because Allie came running up and told me that Caleb was stuck on top of the batting cage. When I got back, the game was over, and we had lost. And Diane was heart broken.

That Saturday, I took Diane over to the grandparents to help Grandma clean house; she'd been doing this for a while. Grandma couldn't sweep or mop or bend over much, so she paid Diane. I just dropped her off because I knew Grandma would be busy cleaning and Grandpa was busy with the dish installer. They had seen the channels one of their friends got with a dish and immediately set out to get one of their own. I dropped Diane off and watched her go in the front door; then, I started for home. I hadn't driven over three blocks when my cell phone rang and Diane asked breathlessly if I would come back in a hurry; she needed me. I turned around, drove back to their house, pulled into the driveway, and parked. Diane was waiting on the porch. She was bubbling with excitement.

I climbed the front steps and she came over, hugged me, and whispered, "Look out back at the guy that's putting in the dish." She looked around to see if anyone else were listening. "I think he's my daddy."

"How do you know?" I asked because I knew she'd never seen her father.

"He looks like him. My mamma told me what he looked like." I followed her through the house, stopping long enough to kiss Grandma on the cheek. We went to the very back of the house and looked out a window onto my grandparents' very large back yard. I saw my grandfather's slightly stooped, gray haired form. Next to him was a chubby blond man who was red-faced from the exertion of putting in the dish. No. He did look like Diane's father, but it wasn't him.

"I'm sorry, baby," I said, hugging her to me, "that's not him."

"Oh," she said and even though I couldn't see her face, I thought she might be about to cry. I hugged her tighter. "Do you think I'll ever meet him?" she asked.

"I wish I knew." Honesty was the only way with something like this. "Do you want me to wait for you?"

"Uh hunh," she said, nodding affirmatively, but not looking up at me.

"I'll be right here," I said, and she went back to the front of the house to help Grandma, sighing deeply. I sat down and watched the dish installer put the finishing touches on their satellite dish under the watchful eye of my grandfather. That dish guy almost had a wonderful girl as his daughter. His loss. It's kind of funny how everyone you meet can somehow impact your life. It's kind of funny how a child can hurt so much and keep right on breathing.

The Lauderdale County Juvenile Detention Facility. This was one place I thought I'd never visit. Yellow cushions. Ugly, yellow cushions. Uncomfortable, ugly, yellow cushions. The kind of cushions that stick to you when you try to get up. Which makes sense because you don't want it to be a friendly, inviting place. Mamma was sitting next to me, clutching her purse for dear life; there were some other parents in this place who were definitely on the other side of the law. How on earth did we arrive here? I wasn't sure.

No, that wasn't right. The short answer was that Caleb keyed a car; the long answer was that he stopped taking his medicine. He was feeling okay and didn't see why he had to keep taking it. And we didn't catch it. Mamma or I would remind him to take it every morning (and again every evening), and he would walk into the kitchen and look like he took his pill; he even complained that the medicine gave him a stomachache or kept him awake at night, both known side effects. The charade continued until Mamma was going to call in a refill for both of his prescriptions and found both bottles almost full. Who knows when he actually stopped? That was Sunday.

On Monday, which was the first official day of summer for the kids and with Trisha graduating this coming Friday night, I took Caleb to the Community Mental Health Center to see the doctor, because we were concerned about the medicine issue, while Mamma ran to the school to pick up everyone's report cards. I had Caleb up there by 8 a.m. and we got in pretty quickly. Caleb went into the doctor's office for some "counseling" and came back out in five minutes with a new prescription. All during the trip home, I tried to explain why it was important for him to take his medicine daily whether he felt bad or not, and that keeping the medicine in his system was what was important. I also asked him if the doctor had talked to him, and Caleb said no; the doctor had talked to someone on the phone, asked Caleb if he was okay, and handed him the prescription.

We got back home and walked into the house to find Mamma sitting at the kitchen table. With Caleb's report card. He failed. Caleb didn't believe it. He insisted on reading every word on the report card, which included lots of zeroes for homework grades and two in-school suspensions that we knew nothing about, and then calling the school to ask them if they were sure. Of course, he was mad at me because somehow I let this happen even though I was the one helping him with that homework that he didn't turn in. And he was mad at Mamma because she didn't look in his book bag to see that he didn't turn stuff in and then force him to.

"This ain't right! They're lyin. I turned some of that stuff in," he said.

"But not enough apparently," I said.

"They're wrong; they told me I passed," he insisted.

"Caleb, why would they tell you that and then send this?" Mamma said, pointing at the report card he'd thrown back on the kitchen table.

"I can go to summer school," he said.

"No, you can't. We can't afford it," I said. "And both Mawmaw and I have been telling you this would happen if you didn't do your work."

"All my friends passed," he said, face contorting as he began to cry.

"Yes, they probably did," I agreed.

"They have Mammas and Daddies who love them."

"And you have an uncle and a grandmother who love you," I said.

"It ain't the same."

"No, it ain't. But you didn't fail because of that. You failed because you didn't try. You know that."

"I'm not smart like you," he said in a accusatory tone of voice.

"I'm not talking about me; I'm talking about you. You've got to finish high school and go to college. Do you want to have nothing all of your life?"

"I want to be with my friends," he said.

"You'll see them; you'll just be a year behind them," I said, trying to convince him, and me, that this wasn't the end of the world even though that's what it felt like.

"It's not fair."

"What did you expect would happen?" I asked, really curious to know.

"I dunno," he said, giving me just the answer I had expected.

"Go to your room for a while; we'll talk more later."

"I'm not going back to that school."

"Caleb, we've got all summer. Don't start this."

"I'm not. I won't go. I'll run away."

"Where will you go?"

"To see my Mamma."

"You might see her, but you won't stay with her. You know how she is."

"Then I'll go somewhere else."

"You'll still have to go to school, wherever you go."

"I won't."

"Caleb. Stop. You know you're gonna go to school. Do you want people to say you're ignorant?"

"It's better than being a faggot!"

"Caleb," Mamma said.

"Anything's better than being a faggot," he continued, sullenly, "You make me sick!"

I just looked at him standing there and said, "Maybe so," and turned to go in the bedroom we shared, sitting on the foot of the bed and turning on the television, channel surfing, pressing the remote so hard it made my fingers hurt.

Two hours later the sheriff came. They had a warrant for Caleb's arrest. For keying a boy's car a week before. At church. During the after school program I had allowed him to go to. Caleb and another boy had keyed both sides of the car while it was parked in front of a very large window where all of the other kids were standing and watching, so they could report it to the sheriff. Part of me wanted to say that for god's sake if you were going to do something illegal you definitely wanted to do it where no one could see you. And the kid whose car that he keyed is one of the nicest young men at his school.

The sheriff handcuffed Caleb and led him out to the patrol car. Caleb was so scared, he'd turned white. I thought he was going to faint. Mamma, Allie, Diane, and I walked out with him. Cat jumped up and tried to lick him on the face. Diane asked the sheriff if she could hug Caleb, and the sheriff said okay. Then Allie hugged him, and Mamma; I didn't hug him, but I did put my hand on his shoulder and give it a squeeze. The sheriff gave us a piece of paper telling us that Caleb would appear in court on Friday morning at 9 o'clock and that he would be remanded to the detention facility until then.

Which brings us back to the ugly yellow cushions that were on the chairs just past the metal detector. We had come up here Tuesday morning to meet with the counselor, but we didn't come into this area. The counselor had given us a list of supplies that Caleb would need: a four roll pack of toilet paper, toothpaste, toothbrush, comb, soap, shampoo – all had to have his name on them in permanent marker. The counselor also said that one of us could visit him on Thursday afternoon between the hours of 1:30 – 4:00 p.m. for fifteen minutes. Mamma wanted to be the one to visit, so I had her back up here right at 1:30 Thursday. She was back out promptly at 1:45, and I could tell she'd been crying.

"How is he?" I asked; I had wanted to go but I knew Caleb would want Mamma more than me.

"Scared. He says he hasn't slept at all," she said, wiping her eyes on a Kleenex she'd gotten from the counselor. "He's afraid the other inmates will steal his clothes and stuff."

"Did you tell him we'd be back up here tomorrow morning?"

"Yeah. He said to tell everyone that he loved them," she said, then she laughed a little, "Even you."

On Friday, the judge told Caleb he was a fool to hang around people who would get him in trouble. She also said he had the worst attitude of any kid she'd had up there in a very long while. Caleb and the other boy (both in stylish orange jumpsuits that perfectly matched their handcuffs) admitted keying the car, so all she had to do was give the sentence: six months probation during which time if he got in trouble for anything, he'd spend the remainder of the sentence in the detention facility, $2,846 (half to be paid by each defendant) to repaint the car- more than the car was actually worth, twenty hours of community service, and a letter of apology to be sent to the court who would then forward it to the offended party. I wanted to be an offended party. After the sentencing, we took a very tired, hungry, subdued Caleb home.

50

Time does have a way of getting away from you, especially the older you get; it's just funny the way time goes sometimes.

I've been working at this college for over ten years. How did that happen? One day, I'll have been here long enough to end up in charge of everything (and then heads will definitely roll). As I looked at the new innocent teachers ready for the slaughter, I remembered my wide-eyed first days here. The woman who had been assigned as my mentor had looked me up and down in a serious fashion and said, "Stick with me, kid! I know where all of the bodies are buried." And I truly believed that there must be a storage facility somewhere on campus where we did indeed put the bodies of those students who stubbornly refused, when faced with the onslaught of professionals educated in all of the modern teaching methodology, to learn anything.

Now I got to be the mentor. I tell my mentees to enjoy the good moments and grit their teeth through the bad moments. Those would eventually end. And keep good records. Sometimes these young adults had to be tricked into learning, and they resented it, but one day they'd come back and thank you. Expect delayed gratification. And finally, by golly, you had better be able to laugh. A lot and hard. Life appreciates it; teachers need it.

My Trisha would be here next semester. A freshman. That was hard to believe too. She just couldn't be that old. My Trisha. That was how I thought of all of the kids privately. My Trisha. My Megan. My Caleb.

My Allie. My Diane. My heroes. My reason for everything. When did that change of thought happen? I was not sure.

But Trisha had been the first. And probably the reason for everything else. I had been there when she was born just before I began my adventure overseas; I was there when my mother threw a fit about the roaches in the old Matty Hersey Hospital, the hospital for those who could afford no where else, and we took Trisha home six hours after she was born. I wasn't working at the time, so I stayed home with Lynn because Trisha's father was already long gone. Lynn and I would run in the bedroom every few minutes to make sure the baby was breathing. And Trisha would fall asleep on my chest listening to my heart beat. I was working overseas when Megan, Caleb, Allie, and Diane were born, so I didn't quite have the same connection to them. Trisha had always been my baby. My feelings for the others crystallized later. It was because she told me she was hungry all the time and she told me how to smoke crack – she'd seen her mother doing it- that my mother and I had decided to take them. I didn't know what else to do. Maybe they would have been better off in foster care. But I couldn't have lived with myself if that had happened. My mind just automatically goes to the worst case scenario, or it loops into hysterical fantasy.

Trisha didn't have a good childhood. I can't remember the number of times I didn't remember to pick her up after school, and she would call and say, "Ya'll forgot me again" in a little voice- the beginning of my guilt. Or the number of birthday parties that none of her friends, if you could call them that, came to. Of course, it had nothing to do with the fact that these parties were hastily arranged affairs – memory again – and often the invitations were given out the day before – or the day of. I learned though. And now I might not remember exactly whose birthday is in this month, but I know it has to be someone's. Small steps. Somehow, and I really don't know how, Trisha persevered. The cost of her perseverance was an intense internalization. No one could see how much she hurt. But because of her, the other kids had it a bit easier, and I learned a little through her disappointments.

She graduated on June 12, at 6 p.m. All of the kids, my mother and I were there. My sister Sara and her daughter Mckenna were there. My grandparents were there to see their eldest great-grandchild accept her diploma. Trisha's boyfriend was there. Everyone sat down on the first row of bleachers. I couldn't bring myself to sit right then; I wanted to take more of it in, so I went to the top of the bleachers. It was a beautiful night. Absolutely gorgeous as only a summer night in the South can be. The almost full moon was so bright that only a few lights were needed. The stars seemed to twinkle feverishly. There was just enough breeze to keep the heat from becoming overpowering. I watched four generations of my family; Megan all blonde and sitting straight-backed in the way only a young girl on the threshold of great beauty can, Caleb, Allie and Diane were all fidgety, as was Grandpa, the very old and the very young do have a lot in common. Grandma had on a bright purple pant suit that was giving the moon a run for its money; it was the same one she wore – and I begged my mother to tell her not to – to my college graduation. Grandma was always a product of the Depression; she had a certain price that she would pay for anything – from clothes to a hair cut and permanent – and she absolutely, positively would not under any circumstances go above it. Bargain bins were her life. And she'd managed to put away quite a lot of money that way.

And, after the graduation had begun, Lynn was there. We didn't expect her. My mother had told her not to come if she was drinking or if she brought her boyfriend Chris or her other boyfriend Bud; they both conveniently lived in the same trailer park and she vacillated between. She looked better than I'd seen her look in a long time. I don't think anyone else saw her; if they did, they've never mentioned it. Her hair was combed, and she was wearing makeup. Of course, she brought Chris; he looked like he might fall down if the wind hit him right (heroin chic). He was in dirty jeans, a hole infested t-shirt and a baseball cap turned backwards. I was really surprised that he was there, not only because of what Mamma had told Lynn but because I'd heard that she and Chris had been really fighting. She was mad at him because they no longer had sex; he said that she made his dick hurt the last time and adamantly refused any other coital contact. But Lynn was radiant.

She didn't sit with us. She'd abdicated that position and had the presence of mind to realize it. She stood at the fence. Watching. They called Trisha's name, and we all cheered and clapped so hard my hands hurt. Except Lynn. She just watched, clutching the fence as if her life depended on it, so intently. After it was over and new graduates threw their caps in the air (except Trisha because she said she didn't want to have to crawl all over everything trying to find it), everyone got up and went down to the field. Lynn didn't go. I walked over to her. I truly can't stand my sister, but this was neither the time nor the place, so I just said, "Hello." She looked at me and didn't say anything; we both looked at Trisha and the rest of the family who were already out on the field surrounding her like a cocoon.

I looked at Lynn again, and said what I was thinking, "Thank you." It was not a thank you for coming; it was a thank you for giving me the kids and making my life more complete. It was a thank you tinged with bitterness and desperation but ultimately lifesaving. Because I knew that I had lived more, experienced more, felt more than she ever would. She only had the hole where all of that should have been. A hole that she kept trying desperately to fill. She looked at me for what seemed like a long time, not saying anything. I was not even sure if she had heard me. Her eyes were red rimmed and glistened with unshed tears and there was a sad smile on her lips but no words. As if her voice just couldn't be made to work. She reached out and grabbed my arm in a viselike grip; I could feel her heart beating. She pulled me close with a strength I didn't think she had and kissed me on the cheek with her parched lips. Then she let go, motioned for Chris to follow her, and left. I went to join the family and proudly take my place.

51

Caleb Stewart
June 20th 2004
Letter of Apology

Dear James,

I'm sorry for damaging your car. I don't know what I was thinking; you just got me mad and I don't know why I was mad at you but something just made me do what I did to your car because I just really lost it and I went a little over my head and I just want to apologize to you for that; I wont bother you or your stuff again. So I'm sorry for doing that to your car. I knew I shouldn't have done that but I got carried away but now I know not to mess with people's cars because it can get you in a lot of trouble; everybody was telling me to do it and I wasn't at first but they kept on peer pressuring me to do that to your car so I did it but I didn't really touch your car i just barely touched but now I know not to listen to anybody when they tell me to do something; I'll just walk away and ignore them like my uncle is always telling me to. I promise you I didn't mean to key your car; I was just trying to be cool and I was just trying to prove to the other people who told me to do it and who watched me do it. I was just trying to be cool I guess, and that's not a right way to be cool; I just wanted to say that I am sorry okay. I know we used to be friends before all this stuff happened but I know not to do anything like that again and I know if I was you then I would have done the same thing you're doing because I wouldn't want anybody touching my car. Is there any way you can forgive me for what I did to your car because all I want is to be friends with everybody and not have enemies and that's a good way to have enemies. I'm sorry and I won't do it again, okay? I know it was so stupid of me to do that to your car, but I just wanted attention, that's all. I didn't get any good attention, though, I just got in trouble. That's all I have to say to you. I'm sorry for keying your car and if there's anything I can do to make it up to you then tell me and I'll do it okay well I'm sorry and it won't happen again … …

Sincerely,

Caleb Stewart

52

As an erstwhile teaching professional, I have had to endure a very large number of never-ending meetings and lectures. I just love when the college has paid someone an obscene amount of money to speak to us for (a minimum of) three hours in a monotone voice about ways to make the "educational experience" more exciting. Or they will bring slides, a power point presentation, or a handout and then read everything to us. Worth every obscene cent. I teach at a college; I've mastered reading. This is all in an effort to get other erstwhile professionals pepped up for the upcoming semester or year or eternity or to find that "magic bullet" that will once and for all solve or get us out of the educational quagmire of "why the kids aren't learning" which I could only think might have something to do with some of us teaching in the monotone way they present at meetings. But I digress.

As I said, meetings and mind-numbing lectures used to rate, in my world at least, as the worst thing I've ever had to endure. This past week, however, changed all of that. My new definition of worst goes something like this: Take one house, five kids, a mother, then take away the power, phone, computer. Add to it rain, hurricane force winds and trees falling all over creation and beyond. Then stir.

When the news said that the weather would get bad, I didn't really give it a lot of thought. This is Mississippi; it happens all the time. I was wrong. Our power went off at 4:13 a.m. Thursday. We woke up to a hot house and a leaking, smelly refrigerator. And no phone. Even cell phones were iffy, but we were able to make a brief call to the grandparents. Grandma answered and said they were fine, but even if they weren't, they were okay with God and that was all that was important. Then the phone went dead. And we had no cable; that hurt the most. The kids, my mother and I just looked at each other and tried not to mention the ever-increasing smell coming from the house and our bodies. We napped a lot. About three p.m. Thursday afternoon, Megan decided to take a shower. Since we are completely electric, there was no hot water but she decided to be a brave soldier because she wanted to go to the mall, which never lost power, with some guy; she was so strong in adversity. She lit three candles in the bathroom, took a shower, got out, put on make up and then tried to plug in her blow dryer. She ran in the living room and said, "Bruce will be here in ten minutes. What am I going to do?"

This weather proved that neither the kids nor I came from hardy pioneer stock. Caleb just kept looking at me and saying, "Do you think the T.V. works?"

I just looked right back at him and said, "Why don't you try it and see?" I was so tired of explaining.

Later that afternoon, my mother decided to take the kids and drive in to see the grandparents who, as it happens, had not lost power or anything; it must be their good living. Everyone left, and I sat in the living room alone, except for the two inside dogs, Belle and Buster; it was not often that I was actually by myself in my house, so I decided that the time was right for a hardy Chardonnay and a brisk loofah. Then I remembered that there was no hot water, and the Chardonnay might be a bit warm. Who cared? I got that bottle out and proceeded to imbibe to my heart's content.

After about half of the bottle was gone, I got it in my head to scare Mamma and the kids when they got back. I found an old sheet that I planned to throw over me and jump out of the bushes when they pulled up the driveway. I got that big old sheet out and went outside to sit in the bushes next to the mail box, drink the remainder of my Chardonnay and wait. Cat kept me company, trying to pull my sheet away with his teeth. I listened for them, actually I was listening to the dogs because they always barked when a car came up the road; Cat always started the barking and the inside dogs would take up the chorus until there was no doubt that we were about to have company.

Our house was situated at the top of a hill but right at a sharp tree-lined curve. You really didn't see anybody until they were right up on you.

I sat there and waited and drank, and waited and drank, and I kind of lost all track of time-actually I was trying to remember a song by the Bay City Rollers. Suddenly Cat started barking and running around, and I could hear the other dogs inside the house like they always do when company comes; I pulled the sheet completely over me and waited, wanting to catch them as they drove by the mail box. The wind was howling, but I managed to keep the sheet on and climb through the bushes right next to the driveway. I hunkered down until I heard the car come up and, just as it was going past the mail box, I jumped out and yelled, "Boo!!" while attempting to flap my arms; I got caught in the sheet and fell over Cat and the bushes, laughing hysterically and still clutching my bottle.

The officer for the Lauderdale County Sheriff's Department just looked at me, rolled down his window, spit some tobacco juice in the grass, and said, "Just wanted to make sure that everyone was safe up here."

"We're fine," I said, still laughing but trying to look sober, and clutching my sheet around me because I couldn't remember what I had on underneath. He didn't ask any questions; he just backed up, turned around, and left.

The next day, I was nursing a bit of a hangover when my mother became obsessed about Lynn and finding out how she had weathered the storm in Crack Central. Mamma's back was hurting, so she'd already taken the kind of medicine with which you were not allowed to operate heavy machinery, and there were trees down everywhere. So guess who got to go?

Lynn lived in a trailer on Hwy 19 South. The kind of place where you immediately clutched whatever money you had in your possession knowing that someone would be by in a minute to take it from you. I got in my car and made my way through the devastation. A couple of times, I had to turn around and find an alternate route as a large tree had fallen across the road. Then I got to Lynn's place. Not a twig was out of place. Crack Central had been spared. I got to the trailer Lynn shared with Chris and knocked on the door that was propped closed. She had been asleep, but I finally heard her hobble to the door, wrestle the board out of the way, and open the door. She just kind of shrugged a hello and turned and hobbled in to the old, dirty couch in the living room. Bud was sleeping on the floor next to the couch, snoring slightly.

I had followed Mamma's directions because I had never been over this trailer before, but I was sure I heard Mamma say that this was Chris', so I asked, "Whose trailer is this?"

"It's Chris'," Lynn said, "Bud just came over during the storm. His trailer's not as good as this one is." She lit a cigarette and continued, "And, yes, he slept right where he is" pointing to the floor, "I don't go for all that three way kinky shit." She took a long, thoughtful drag off of her cigarette, then said, "He's bisexual, you know."

"What?"

"He's bisexual."

"Who?"

"Bud. Ain't you listening?" she stage whispered, "Bud's a bisexual. He loves giving blowjobs more than anything."

"Really?" I said because I couldn't think of anything else.

"How about it?" she asked.

"How about what?"

She sighed and pursed her lips as if I were the stupidest person on the planet and she couldn't believe she had to repeat herself and said, "How about a blowjob from Bud? He always talks about how handsome you are and how he thinks you got a big one." She stopped to pick something off of her tongue with her third finger and thumb, the first two fingers occupied with a cigarette. "He wants me to watch, but that shit dutn't appeal to me."

"Me either. Look, I just came to see how you were doing. I'm gonna go now, okay?"

"Hey, take me to get some smokes first."

She hobbled over to put on her sandals and I said, "Why are you walking so funny?" A question I was hesitant to ask as I didn't know what she would tell me.

"I got a boil on my Cooter bone. Right up in the wrinkle. I about can't stand it," she said. "I've put toothpaste and fingernail polish on it, but nothing works."

"Lynn," I said, "those aren't for boils."

She looked at me with a cut-throat expression and said, "I had to try something. Anything." The she asked, "Well, you gonna run me to the store or what?"

I didn't want to, but I said yes. She put on a frilly little dress that she'd obviously got from a dumpster and off we went to the grocery store on Frontage Road. I walked quickly and Lynn walked a lot slower due to her Cooter boil. But we went in, and I got some bread because it would save me a trip later.

Then we got to the register. Lynn asked the young lady behind the register for some cigarettes. The cashier got two packs and started ringing up that and the bread.

"Those aren't together," Lynn said.

"Yes, they are." I had decided to pay for them; I guess to celebrate everyone surviving the storm.

"If I'd known you were going to pay, I'd a gotten a carton" she said.

The cashier asked, "How'd ya'll make out during the storm?"

"Oh," Lynn said, "I had a little radio, and I played it and danced around the trailer." She was demonstrating some of her dance moves when there was a loud "thwap" sound.

The elderly gentleman a few people behind us in line pointed to the floor at Lynn's feet and said, "Hey! She's trying to steal something! That's why my food bill is so damn high. And me on a fixed income." I looked at where he was pointing, and there was a single piece of bacon with a large band aid stuck to each end.

The cashier just looked at it, then said, "I'd better get the manager."

Lynn said, in a pretty loud voice, "I am not stealing any god-damned bacon! Do you think I'd steal one god-damned piece of bacon by hiding it in my twat? If I was going to steal, I'd take the whole damn pack and believe you me it wouldn't fit down there!"

The man behind us said, "You should try the bacon bits."

"Who are you?" Lynn said, and no one does exasperated quite like she does when she's on her game. Then she turned back to the cashier and said, "I got a boil down there and I heard that bacon fat will help it come to a head."

"Who told you that?" I asked, trying not to laugh, because it really wasn't funny to get arrested for shoplifting.

"Grandma," Lynn replied. I should have known; that sounded like one of her remedies.

The cashier motioned to an officious looking middle aged man who walked over and said, "What's the problem?" She pointed to the bacon on the floor. He looked at it and then looked at us and said, "I better call the police."

The old man said, "I'm a witness. I saw *every* thing." Giving extra emphasis to the next to last word, throwing some senseless suspense into the mix.

"My sister had that on when we came in the store," I said, placatingly, "She has a boil; look, she doesn't even like bacon."

"I do too when it's fried right, not when it's been stuck in my crotch," she said, moving her head around like she was the diva of all divas.

"Look, I guess we'll overlook this this time what with us just having a hurricane and all, but I am gonna have to ask you to leave," the manager said.

"Let me just pay for this stuff," I said, pointing to the bread and cigarettes.

"No, you better leave now," he said.

We left, walked to the car and just sat there. The elderly man who was behind us in line pushed his buggy out and went right in front of my car. He stopped long enough to look at us and thrust up his fist and shake it; then, he went to his car looking thoroughly satisfied with himself.

"We were asked to leave the Piggly Wiggly," Lynn said.

"Yep."

"Some people have no sense of humor."

"True."

"Wanna go to Walmart?" she asked, her eyes twinkling.

I got home later and Mamma asked me, "Is she okay?"

"She's fine," I said, "She's got a boil on her cooter bone, and she told me that Bud wants to give me a blowjob."

Mamma laughed and said, "Last week, she told me that Bud wanted to screw an older woman."

"What did you say?"

"I told her that I loved her dearly, but I wouldn't touch any man who had laid his hand, mouth, or any other part of his anatomy on her. She was very offended."

53

Yesterday was almost, but not really, an okay day. I argued with Caleb about him letting his pants sag around his knees; I understood that this was kids' way of freaking parents out, but I just couldn't stand the thought of my child running around with his ass sticking out. We also argued about shaving. For some odd reason, Caleb shaved his arms and legs to "see what they would look like." To make matters worse, I couldn't get the song "Touch Me in the Morning" out of my head.

Allie had an asthma flare up and this, coupled with the onset of pneumonia, made it to where she couldn't breathe. Mamma took her to the doctor who immediately put her in the hospital. I couldn't stand it. Allie, who skinny people think is too skinny, just looked so helpless in that oxygen tent with the I.V. sticking out of her arms; they thought they would never get it in her arm as Allie has "rolling" veins – this caused a minor disturbance between me and Nurse Beulah because I told her I would hurt her if she kept poking my child. Mamma asked me to leave. Allie was only in there for three days, getting breathing treatments every two hours, and I took the other kids up to see her, nodding cordially to Nurse Beulah as we walked passed. We were fairly certain that she would get out of the hospital Saturday, so I went to bed rather early Friday night. Trisha was staying with her boyfriend. Megan was staying at her friend Brianna's. Diane was at her friend Kayla's. So it was just Caleb and me. Caleb slept in his bed, but I got the two dogs Buster and Belle, all of whom usually sleep with my mother. Belle was a horrible sleeping partner; she absolutely positively had to sleep between my legs.

I have to digress for a moment and to say that I had a few pairs of underwear that have holes in them; the holes were not really noticeable. They were kind of underneath if you know what I mean. There was one pair in particular that was really comfortable. I had been meaning to throw them away for a while, but this was the pair I was wearing.

We went to bed, and I was in deep REM sleep mode when all of the sudden Belle decided to put her cold, wet nose in a place I'm fairly certain was never meant for her cold wet nose. I jumped up, hit my head on the headboard of my bed, and knocked myself out for a good three hours; I obviously needed the extra sleep. I vaguely remembered the phone ringing and my mother telling me to come and pick them up from the hospital. The next thing I recall was finally coming to full consciousness with the phone in my hand.

After picking them up and getting them home, along with approximately $500 worth of medicine not covered by insurance, I had to get Diane from another friend's house. Everyone kept asking me if I was okay because I was pale, and I kept holding the back of my head – the place with the large golf ball sized bump. I kept smiling and (slightly) nodding my head that everything was alright.

Did I mention that a highway patrol officer who obviously didn't know how she drives gave Megan her driver's license and now she could drive anywhere until 10 p.m.? She somehow (and I think my concussion aided her) convinced me to let her drive to tumbling practice; I rode shotgun. It was a very good abdominal/butt workout; I tightened them the entire way to Collinsville. Then I fought with her tumbling/dance teacher. This woman told two of Megan's friends (who are also in the class) to "please talk to Megan about her weight." I was livid. And I said, "Shouldn't you lead by example?"; her teacher wasn't a small woman and didn't take my comment well either. All she had to do was come and talk to us, but no; she had to involve a third and fourth party. Megan had been upset about her weight lately, and now I knew why. I let her drive back (even though I had bargained with God earlier that if he let me live I would never let her drive my car again –I'm sure God understood), and I told her that if she became anorexic or bulimic, I would never forgive her and would remove her name from my will. She said she wouldn't become either, and I didn't have anything she wanted anyway.

<h1 style="text-align:center">54</h1>

"You gotta help me. I can't do this anymore."

A lot changed when Lynn finally uttered those words. My family had been waiting a long time for Lynn to want to change her behavior. Still, no matter how much we wanted it, it was unexpected when it finally happened.

She was talking to Mamma. Lynn had gotten on a talking kick lately. She'd call when she was drunk (which meant it was at all hours) and want to talk to the kids. Mamma and I wouldn't let her do that. She'd call because she was having a panic attack, full-fledged, thinking she had a brain tumor or heart palpations (which then caused her to have heart palpations). Then she'd try to do little things for us; she, Chris and Bud (still together – a heart warming love story of three people, alcohol and crystal meth, and a trailer park) brought us a load of firewood to get us ready for winter. That was very nice of them. When they left, they decided to stop at the end of the road to pick up aluminum cans – a source of ready, steady cash. Our next door neighbor passed them on her way home; she called Mamma and told her to check on the kids because there were some "unsavory characters" down the road. Lynn would also call Sara, or Grandma and Grandpa. Anyone who'd listen and we really started worrying about her brain.

She'd talk to me or Sara and say, "Remember when we used to …" then she'd talk about something that hadn't happened. Or she'd tell me about screwing the drug dealer for a rock or the middle school principal who would come over to her trailer and take nude pictures of her (she claimed from the neck down only) for ten dollars a piece; then she'd forget she'd said anything and when I'd mention how worried we were about what she was doing, she'd say, "I'd never do anything like that. What are you talking about?" She kept getting worse and worse, finally telling Caleb that she was ready to end it all. Mamma chewed her out and told her she could not under any circumstances talk to the kids again.

A month later, a few weeks after Trisha's graduation, she asked for help. Lynn was finally tired of "living her life." And she was very specific; she wanted to go to a place far enough away to keep her "friends" away but near enough that we could visit. And it had to be long term. Thirty or sixty days weren't going to cut it. Mamma and Grandpa called everyone they knew and finally got her "the next available bed" in Whitfield, the state hospital, Gayleen's old haunt. We were ready to try anything.

Mamma took Lynn to the Sheriff's department, so she could sign a court order admitting herself. It cost thirty-eight dollars. We were then told to have her at Whitfield, just outside of Jackson, Mississippi, promptly at 10:30 a.m. Wednesday morning. I decided to go with Mamma to take her. And the next morning, Sara showed up; she'd taken off of work (which Sara simply does not do), so she could go too. She left Mckenna and Belle at our place (They stay there everyday of summer vacation anyway; plus Belle was more our dog now than theirs). We put Trisha and Megan in charge and hoped that most of the kids would stay asleep most of the time we were gone. We left at 7 a.m., so we could stop somewhere over there and get breakfast. I drove, Mamma sat in the passenger seat and Sara and Lynn were in the back. Sara brought a cd of old music the kids had burned for her, and we moved rhythmically to "Shake Your Groove Thing" and "Disco Duck." Is being a nerd nature or nurture?

"Remember when we jumped off the roof of the old house onto the trampoline?"

"I miss that dog. She was the best dog in the world."

"I got so mad you had to sit on me til I calmed down."

"And I hit you with that loaf of bread and bread went all over the kitchen."

"Sara and I put your hand in warm water to make you pee on the bed."

"And Grandma tried to make us eat liver, and we threw it behind the stove when she wasn't looking."

We were kids again, in the car with Mamma on a trip somewhere. When there was nothing in the world outside of the car. Our own universe before the real world trickled in. There was no safer feeling in the world. We stopped at Shoney's for the breakfast buffet, but no one was really hungry. So we sat and continued reminiscing. Lynn started to get nervous (her chain smoking increased) and was worried that they might still give electric shock therapy.

We got to the main gate at a quarter to ten and were directed to the building Lynn would be staying in. Building 81. Mamma, Sara, and I sat outside on a picnic table while they gave her a complete physical. They gave her three shots – one for the cold she had had for over a year and two for gonorrhea. She said we better tell Bud and Chris, and his brother Sam, and the guy in the last trailer on the right. Then she asked if gonorrhea were only transmitted by intercourse. The doctor said no, there were other ways; Lynn said we'd also better tell Alice who runs the fish camp in Lakeland and her son Trent.

A nurse came out and said, "Honey, it's time." Lynn stood up and grabbed her two plastic bags which held her cigarettes, clean underwear – grandma insisted-, three shirts, two pairs of pants, and a few pictures. The nurse said to Mamma, "You know she can't have any visitors or phone calls for the first two months."

Lynn hugged Sara, then me and then Mamma, and said, "I guess I'll be seeing you" and turned to go inside. At the door, she stopped, turned back around, and said, "Don't ya'll forget me in here, okay?" And she was gone.

The trip back was quiet and uneventful. Trisha called to ask when we'd get back 'cause she had to go to work. Megan called because Diane had put on Megan's panties and wouldn't give them back. Mckenna called to say that Belle had just eaten something that looked like cat doodoo. Allie called to say she loved us and could we get everyone a hamburger on our way home? Caleb called to say that he'd accidentally used the dog's shampoo that was left by the tub when Buster was washed yesterday and would it kill him? Completely uneventful.

In my mind's eye, I could see them as adults. The pharmacist, the nurse, the coach (hopefully), the teacher, the exotic dancer. All good humans. Mamma and I have done a good job.

Lynn wrote that her counselor said that the way Lynn's personality was, she would "go from one addiction to another. It may not exactly be alcohol or drugs, it could be gambling, eating, or shopping." She would "find something and become addicted to it." She simply had to "make sure it's a positive addiction like gardening." Lynn the gardener. Maybe one day, Lynn the hero, best not to think too much about that. But it would be so much better than Lynn the addict. Or Lynn the bitch. And there are five acres out here on this damned hill.

Lightning Source UK Ltd.
Milton Keynes UK
UKHW010654020322
399448UK00001B/62